Amanda Cross is the  run,
Avalon Foundation ‍ at
Columbia University. at
Columbia, she has he‍ appointments
and fellowships. Under her real name she has published
studies of David Garnett and Christopher Isherwood, as
well as *Towards Androgyny* (1973), *Reinventing Womanhood*
(1979), *Representation of Women in Fiction* (1982) and *Writing
A Woman's Life* (1989).

She began writing feminist detective stories as Amanda
Cross in 1964 with *In the Last Analysis*, nominated for the
best First Novel by the Mystery Writers of America.
Virago publishes *A Death in the Faculty, No Word from
Winifred, A Question of Max, Sweet Death, Kind Death, The
James Joyce Murder, A Trap for Fools, The Theban Mysteries*
and her most recent novel, *The Players Come Again*.

AMANDA CROSS

POETIC JUSTICE

Published by VIRAGO PRESS Limited 1991
20–23 Mandela Street, Camden Town, London NW1 0HQ

First published in Great Britain by Victor Gollancz Limited
in 1970.
First published in the United States of America
by Avon Books, a division of The Hearst Corporation, New York 1979.

*A CIP catalogue record for this title
is available from the British Library*

Printed in Great Britain by Cox & Wyman Ltd, Reading, Berkshire

Note

It will, of course, be obvious to every reader
that the quotations at the heads of the chapters,
and most of the poetry scattered reverently
throughout this work,
are from the writings of W. H. Auden.
The author is grateful to Faber & Faber Ltd,
for its permission to quote from the
copyrighted works of Mr. Auden
and reprint them here.

Contents

PART ONE

Before Death

PROLOGUE

*though one cannot always
Remember exactly why one has been happy,
There is no forgetting that one was.*

Professor Kate Fansler mounted the stairs to the upper campus where the azalea bushes were just coming into bud. She did not yet know, on that May morning, that the students had already occupied the administration building. Few knew as yet; tomorrow, it would be front-page news around the world. Now she walked past lawns just turning rich with green. The students, damn them, were trampling thoughtlessly across the new grass, heedless of all the cautionary signs and fences erected by the University's tireless gardeners. The annoyance she had always felt at this desecration had grown, if anything, more acute with the years. She reprimanded herself for crotchetiness. " '. . . unready to die,' " Kate thought, " 'but already at the stage when one starts to dislike the young.' " The lines were Auden's and, as always, they gave Kate special pleasure. She·was going that afternoon to see him receive a gold medal for poetry.

Kate had never met Auden and was unlikely ever to do so. Yet there had existed between them for over ten years what she considered to be the perfect relationship. That it was wholly satisfactory to Auden was to be inferred from the fact that he had never heard of it; its satisfactions for Kate rested securely on the knowledge that he never would. Auden's private person did not interest her. But, over the years, his poetry and such delightful facts about him as appeared in books by his friends had given her a new awareness of life. She had never read a word of criticism or scholarship about him and, safely and professionally ensconced as she was in the Victorian period, planned never to do so. Which just goes to show, as, indeed, did everything happening that day, that foresight is not a human attribute. At that very moment the students had opened the President's files and begun to read his letters.

> *Abruptly mounting her ramshackle wheel,*
> *Fortune has pedalled furiously away;*

but Kate, who did not know that, sat down and pleasurably regarded the newly blossomed tulips.

Kate had first seen Auden a decade before on a television program which, since she did not own a set, she had gone to considerable inconvenience to catch. (Her hosts had been more inconvenienced still, since the program had begun at nearly midnight and went on into the small hours of the morning; abandoning Kate, Auden, and their living room, they had finally gone to bed.) Kate could no longer remember the occasion for the program, nor exactly what Auden and the others had been discussing, but she did remember that throughout the long hours Auden had called loudly and unsuccessfully for tea: apparently as difficult to obtain in a television studio as Coca-Cola in a four-star Parisian restaurant. Kate had never forgotten Auden's frown. Reportedly, he had been frowning since boyhood. "I see him," Christopher Isherwood had written, "frowning as he sings opposite me in the choir, surpliced, in an enormous Eton collar, above which his great red flaps of ears stand out, on either side of his narrow, scowling, pudding-white face." They had been at school together: Isherwood was to present Auden with his gold medal that afternoon.

"And so, after all these years, I am forcibly evicted from my office. They have taken over the College building too."

"Who has?" Kate stared at the man standing beside her.

"Fate," Frederick Clemance observed, "has, I see, granted you some additional moments of blessed ignorance. And what were you thinking of, sitting there contemplating tulips?"

"Auden," Kate said.

"You don't say?" Clemance sat down beside her on the bench. "Do you know his poetry well?"

"I browse in it," Kate admitted, "as though it were a meadow." She regarded Clemance with a certain degree of discomfort. She had admired him for years, had studied with him as a graduate student (which for a woman had been a singular honor indeed), had followed with interest and devotion his growing reputation—he was now one of the University's luminaries. She was, indeed, technically speaking, his colleague, but she had never before chatted with him.

"There they go, you see. Crawling around the ledges like so many monkeys and shouting obscenities. If you come close enough, they will spit down on you. Can it be a new form of panty-raid? At least," Clemance added, "no one ever before involved me in that sort of escapade."

By standing on the bench they could indeed see the students, mostly bearded, and looking, even at that distance, unwashed, posed out the windows, hanging on the bars. "Perhaps, Miss Fansler," Clemance said, climbing down, "you could do me a favor." Kate smiled nervously. So, she imagined, Frederick the Great might have spoken to one of his courtiers.

"If I can, of course," she said.

"It's about Auden."

Kate stared at him blankly. Neither of them, of course, knew yet that their world had changed. For them, the academic machine was still grinding on. Had anyone suggested then to Kate or Clemance that they would soon see their colleagues obscenely mocked by students and clubbed by policemen, they would have questioned his competence. We shared, Kate would think later, a last hour of innocence.

"I am directing a dissertation on Auden; it's finished, actually; the work of a brilliant young man who's eager to have the dissertation examination soon. Professor Pollinger is also on the committee. I was about to look for someone to take over in the final stages, because of all the pressures I'm under. You see how lucky I am to have found you. Do you know Auden?"

"No," Kate said. "And I've never approached his work academically. I really don't feel qualified."

"You'll do beautifully. Knowing Auden, I've never been able to feel properly academic about his work either. I'll tell them at the English Office. Many thanks; I shall be off now and see where all this is leading. I am glad, in more ways than one, that we have met before the tulips." He smiled and walked away. And indeed, in the next day or two, the academic machine, not yet sputtering, ground out an official notice to Kate: "Title of Dissertation: The Poetry of W. H. Auden; Name of Candidate: R. E. G. Cornford; Chairman of Dissertation Committee: Professor Fansler."

By two thirty that afternoon the students had taken a third building and delivered a series of ultimatums to the President of the University who, as usual, was somewhere else. Rumor announced that he was flying home. Meanwhile, the faculty had begun to meet in groups, discussing what action they might take. The Vice-President, temporarily in charge, began to talk of calling the police. Kate hailed a taxi and asked to be driven to the American Academy of Arts and Letters.

But she was not to see Auden in person; that much was immediately clear. At the annual ceremonies of the American Academy of Arts and Letters, the members, and those who are to receive awards or be inducted into member-

6

ship, sit on the stage in numbered seats. The programs held by the audience contain a diagram of the stage indicating who is to occupy each seat. Neither Auden nor Isherwood was there. At the end of the program, Mr. Glenway Wescott agreed to read both Isherwood's speech presenting the gold medal to Auden and Auden's acceptance of it.

The audience was disappointed, but Kate, seated in the balcony, was strangely satisfied; it had always been their words she cared for, not their presences. Isherwood's short speech spoke of "the transformation of seven-year-old Auden Minor into the sixty-one-year-old poet whom we honor today," and ended with Isherwood's taking "advantage of his non-presense to tell him how very proud I am to be his friend." "Dear Christopher," Auden's acceptance speech began; and then: "For me, poetry is firstly a game." Which, Kate thought, listening to the voice of Mr. Wescott, is why we can allow him to be profound. Who but Auden could have written so fine a poem about his bedroom:

Don Juan needs no bed, being far too impatient to undress,
nor do Tristan and Isolde, much too in love to care
for so mundane a matter, but unmythical
mortals require one, and prefer to take their clothes off
if only to sleep.

It was, in fact, an odd poem for Kate to have thought of—had she, perhaps, possessed that day unrecognized prophetic powers? For at her university no one was to undress and go to sleep for an entire week. By the time Mr. Cornford's dissertation arrived at her office, Kate was far too tired even to resent on Auden's behalf the hand of academe.

CHAPTER
ONE

Though mild clear weather
Smile again on the shire of your esteem
And its colors come back, the storm has changed you:
You will not forget, ever,
The darkness blotting out hope, the gale
Prophesying your downfall.

That classes at the University began, as they were scheduled to, on September 17, was a matter of considerable astonishment to everyone. There was not a great deal to be said for revolutions—not, at any rate, in Kate's opinion —but they did accustom one to boredom in the face of extraordinary events, and a pleasant sense of breathless surprise at the calm occurrence of the expected. Kate said as much to Professor Castleman as they waited for the elevator in Lowell Hall.

"Well," he answered, "I might have found myself even more overcome with amazement if they had not managed to put my course in historical methods, which never has less than a hundred and fifty students, into a classroom designed to hold ninety only if the students sit two in a chair, which, these days, they probably prefer to do. Though come to think of it," he added as the elevator, empty, went heedlessly past, apparently on some mysterious mission of its own, "I don't know why students should expect seats at lectures, since audiences can no longer expect them at the theater. We went to a play last night—

I use the word 'play,' you understand, to describe what we expected to see, not what we saw—and not only were there no seats, the entertainment principally consisted of the members of the cast removing their clothes and urging, gently of course, that the audience do likewise. My wife and I, fully clothed, felt rather like missionaries to Africa insufficiently indoctrinated into the antics of the aborigines. Shall we walk down? One thing at least has *not* changed in this university: the elevators. They have never worked, they do not now work, and though an historian should never speak with assurance of the future, I am willing to wager that they never will. Where are you off to? Don't tell me, I know. A meeting. What's more, I can tell you what you are going to discuss: relevance."

"That," said Kate, "would be the expected. As a matter of fact, I have a doctoral examination: the poetry of W. H. Auden. He wrote a good bit of clever poetry to your muse."

"Mine? Gracious, have I got a muse? Just what I've needed all these years. Do you think I could trade her in for a cleaning woman, three days a week with only occasional ironing? My wife would be prostrate with gratitude."

"Trade Clio in? Impossible. It is she into whose eyes 'we look for recognition after we have been found out.' "

"Did Auden write that? Obviously he's never been married. That's a description of any wife. I thought you were in the Victorian period."

"I am, I am. Auden was born in 1907. He only missed Victoria by six years. And don't be so frivolous about Clio. Auden called her 'Madonna of silences, to whom we turn When we have lost control.' "

"Well, get hold of her," Professor Castleman said. "I'm ready to turn."

The dissertation examination was not, in fact, scheduled

for another hour. Kate wandered back toward her office, not hurrying, because no sooner would she reach Baldwin Hall, in which building dwelt the Graduate English Department, than she would be immediately accosted, put on five more committees, asked to examine some aspect of the curriculum about which she knew nothing (like the language requirement for medieval studies) and to settle the problems of endlessly waiting students concerning, likely as not, questions not only of poetry and political polarization, but of pot and the pill as well. Kate strolled along in the sort of trance to which she had by now grown accustomed. It was the result of fatigue, mental indigestion, a sense of insecurity which resembled being tossed constantly in a blanket as much as it resembled anything, and, strangest of all, a love for the University which was as irrational as it was unrewarded.

She would have been hard put to say, she thought looking about her, what it was she loved. Certainly not the administration (had there been one, which, since they had resigned one by one like the ten little Indians, there wasn't). Not the Board of Governors, a body of tired, ultraconservative businessmen who could not understand why a university should not be run like a business or a country club. The students, the faculty, the place? It was inexplicable. The love one shares with a city is often a secret love, Camus had said; the love for a university was apparently no less so.

"Kate Fansler!" a voice said. "How very, very nice. 'I *must* telephone Kate,' I have said to Winthrop again and again, 'we must have lunch, we must have dinner, we must meet.' And now, you see, we have."

Kate paused on the steps of Baldwin Hall and smiled at the sight of Polly Spence. Talk of the unexpected! Polly Spence belonged to the world of Kate's family—she had actually been, years ago, a protégée of Kate's mother's— and there emanated from her the aura of St. Bernard's

—where her sons had gone to school—and Milton Academy, the Knickerbocker dancing classes and cotillions.

"I know," Polly Spence said, "my instincts tell me that if I wait here patiently you will say something, perhaps even something profound, like 'Hello.'"

"It's good to see you, Polly," Kate said. "I don't know what's become of me. I feel like the heroine of that Beckett play who is buried up to her neck and spends every waking moment rummaging around in a large, unorganized handbag. Come to see the action, as the young say?"

"Action? Profanity, more likely. Four-letter-word-bathroom, four-letter-word-sex, and really too tiresome, when I think that my own two poor lambs were positively *glared* at if they said 'damn.' It's not an easy world to keep up with."

"But if I know you, you're keeping up all the same."

"Of course I am. I'm taking a doctorate. In fact, I've almost got it. Now what do you think of that? I'm writing a dissertation for the Linguistics Department on the history of Verner's Law. Please look impressed. The Linguistics Department is overjoyed, because the darlings didn't know there was anything new to say about Verner's Law until I told them, and they've been taking it like perfect angels."

Kate smiled. "I always suspected an extraordinary brain operating behind all your committee-woman talents, but whatever made you decide to get a Ph.D.?"

"Grandchildren," Polly said. "Three chuckling little boys, one gurgling little girl, all under three. It was either hours and hours of baby-sitting, to say nothing of having the little darlings cavalierly *dumped* upon us at the slightest excuse, *or* I had to get a job that would be absolutely respected. Winthrop has encouraged me. 'Polly,' he said, 'if we are not to find ourselves changing diapers every blessed weekend, you had better find something demanding to say you're *doing*.' The children, of course, are furious, but I am now a teaching assistant, very, very busy, thank you, and only condescending to rally round at Christmas and Easter. Summers I dash off to do research and Winthrop joins me when he can. But you look tired, and here I am chatting away. Let's have lunch one day at the Cosmopolitan Club."

"I'm not a member."

"Of course not, dear, though I never understood why. Why *are* you looking so tired?"

"Meetings. Meetings and meetings. We are all trying, as you must have heard, to restructure the University, another way of saying that we, like the chap in the animated cartoons, have looked down to discover we are not standing on anything. Then, of course, we fall."

"But everybody's resigned. The President. The Vice-President. We've got an Acting President, we're getting a Faculty Senate, surely everything's looking up."

"Perhaps. But the English Department has discovered there is no real reason for most of the things they have been happily doing for years. And the teaching assistants —where, by the way, are you being a teaching assistant? Don't tell me the College has reformed itself sufficiently to be hiring female, no-longer-young ladies, however talented . . ."

"Not them; not bloody likely. I'm at the University College. *Very* exciting. Really, Kate, you have no idea."

Kate, looking blank, realized she hadn't.

"Really," Polly Spence said, "the snobbery of you people in the graduate school! We're doing *splendid* work over there . . ."

"Didn't the University College used to be the extension school? Odd courses for people at loose ends like members of labor unions who only work twenty hours a week and housewives whose children are . . . ?"

"That was a hundred years ago. There are no more courses in basket-weaving. We give a degree, we have a chapter of Phi Beta Kappa, and our students are *very* intelligent people who simply don't want to play football or have a posture picture taken."

"Forgive me, Polly. As one always does when one speaks from ignorance and prejudice, I'm sounding a lousy snob."

"Well, you'll be hearing more from us, just you wait and see. Meanwhile, you must come and have dinner. When I tell Winthrop I've met you, he'll insist. He always finds you so entertaining, like Restoration comedy."

"And about as up-to-date. I'm faltering, Polly. If you want to know the truth, I'm thinking of taking up bridge, if not palmistry, astrology, and the finer points of ESP. One of my students has offered to introduce me to a medium with electronic thought waves."

"There is no question about it," Polly said. "We must have lunch at the Cosmopolitan Club. It reassures one."

Kate, walking up the stairs of Baldwin, waved a dismissive hand.

"Kafka," Mark Everglade said, meeting her in the hall outside her office, "where is thy sting?"

"I take it," Kate said, "that is a perpetually appropriate remark these days."

"Perpetually. Would you mind teaching a text course next year in the novels of Bulwer-Lytton?"

"You have to be joking. And what, while I'm doubled over with hilarity, is a text course?"

"One that uses books, of course. I know we're all tired on the first day of the semester, Kate, but surely you could have seen that. You remember books? They're what we used to read before we began discussing what we ought to read. The students have spent the entire summer reforming our course offerings, and it's now to be text courses."

"I have never read Bulwer-Lytton. I have never even discussed reading Bulwer-Lytton, except with some strange student who used to turn up every seven years with another thousand pages on the development of the historical novel. Ah, I see, *The Last Days of Pompeii* is now considered relevant. Perhaps it is, at that."

"If only," Mark Everglade said, "a volcano would come and cover us all with dust. We have done away, as you would have known if you had ever listened at all those meetings this last summer, with lectures and seminars. We now have text courses, preferably in texts nobody ever heard of before, like Bulwer-Lytton and the literature of the emerging African nations. While I think of it, we are in the market for someone who reads Swahili, if you should ever hear of such a person."

"So mysterious," Kate said. "No doubt there are scads of fascinating literary works in Swahili. But I spoke just the other night to someone returned from Africa. He said that in Ethiopia, for example, there are seventy-five different dialects, and that the tribes can only converse with each other in English. In Nigeria, I understand, there are two hundred and twenty-five languages, with English again the common tongue for conversation. Why don't we train people to teach English in Swahili, instead of training people to teach Swahili in English, or is that a particularly reactionary observation?"

"Not only reactionary," Mark said, "but probably in itself grounds for occupying this whole building. Now as to the catalogue . . ."

"Why are we discussing next year's catalogue on this year's first day of classes?"

"As you will see when you meet with the student-faculty committee for finalizing the revisions of the catalogue, everyone keeps changing his mind, so that we've got to get the damn catalogue for next year into print so that no one can change it and we can argue about the year after."

"I am not on the student-faculty committee to finalize anything, and I will not serve on any committee with so barbaric a word as 'finalize' in its title, and that's final," Kate said.

"The title is open to discussion," Mark said, "but I'm afraid you've absolutely got to be on the committee because you've been on it all summer and are the only one who knows what's going on."

" 'We have no means of learning what is really going on.' Auden says."

"I had no idea Auden was so relevant; the ultimate compliment."

"Well, he may be," Kate said, "but I'm not. Do you think that could be my whole problem?"

"It's the problem all right. We are not only magnificently irrelevant, but are prevented, mysteriously, from enjoying the fruits of irrelevance, which are frivolity and leisure."

"I wish I were an African nation," Kate said. "It must be so comforting to think of oneself as emerging."

Kate had time only to dive into her office, add the mail she had collected from her box downstairs to that already on her desk unopened, grab the dissertation on Auden, tell three students who appeared from nowhere that she was *not* having office hours or consultations of any sort, and listen, with perfect impassivity, to the ringing of her telephone. Kate did not claim to have learned much during the previous spring's disruption or the summer's hard committee work, but she had learned one thing: it is not necessary to answer one's telephone. One can always suppose that one is not there. This vaguely existential decision meant, therefore, that Kate avoided for another two and one half hours what her governess used to call a rendezvous with destiny. A nice phrase. But Kate had early on discovered (though considerably after the reign of the governess) that one cannot 'avoid' a destined rendezvous. Rendezvous are either inevitable or impossible.

It was by no means usual for the dissertation examination, the final examination for the degree of Doctor of Philosophy, to be held on the first day of classes. In fact, like so much else now going on, it was hitherto unheard of. But the spring revolutions had meant the inevitable postponement of many doctoral dissertation examinations, partly because the Committee of Seven appointed by the Dean of the Graduate Faculties could rarely be collected (most of them were either wrestling with plainclothesmen at the time, examining identification at the University gates, or begging the mayor to intervene in the University's problems). And even had it been possible to get all seven in one place, it was not possible to find the place. The head of the Graduate English Department, a man for whom, Kate had decided over the summer, the term 'longsuffering' was meiosis, had held several examinations in his living room (to the evident distress of his children, who had planned to watch television at the same time), but after a while all such efforts were given up. When it reached the point where one examination committee (which fortunately included no lady members) met in the men's room of the Faculty Club, and two of those who had been asked at the last minute to serve had never, it soon became evident, heard of the subject under discussion, the office of the Dean of Graduate Faculties declared itself officially closed. For one thing, with all the student raids on the administration buildings, the secretarial staff became so unnerved at the necessity of shoving all records and dissertations into the safe at the threat of occupation that they flatly refused even to come to the office until things had "quieted down."

Today four members of the examining committee had shown up, which was a quorum, and an enormous relief to Kate and the candidate, who had flown in from his teaching post in California especially for the examination. All is, thank God, minimally official, Kate thought, taking her place as chairman at the head of the table. To Kate's right sat the other member of her department, Peter Packer Pollinger, the official sponsor of the dissertation. To her left sat the two necessary representatives of other departments, Professor Kruger from the German Department, and, next to him, Professor Chang from the Department of Asian Civilization. Professor Chang was present as the result of total desperation, but someone else outside the English Department was required, and, after all, Auden, together with Christopher Isherwood, had gone to China in 1938 and written a book about it. The Department of Asian Civilization had told Kate that Professor Chang had never been to China, but one couldn't ask for everything in outside examiners.

All began properly enough. Kate asked Mr. Cornford to leave the room and told the committee what facts about Mr. Cornford, provided in a special folder by the office of the Dean of Graduate Faculties, seemed relevant: his education, present position, date and subject of his master's essay. "Perhaps, then, we can ask the candidate in for the examination," Kate hopefully said.

"Clarification, please," said Professor Chang.

"I beg your pardon," Kate said. "I didn't mean to seem to be rushing. Is there a question about Mr. Cornford? About Auden?"

"Please. I have read dissertation with great interest and attention. But I would like to point out I am not from Department of Asian Civilization. I am from School of Engineering."

"Engineering?" Kate said faintly. "I'm afraid there must be some confusion."

"Mr. Auden is most interesting writer," Professor Chang said, "but are there many limestone landscapes in China?"

"Limestone landscapes!" Professor Kruger said. "It is more a question of the Weimar Republic. Auden does not

realize that the love of death and the rejection of authority . . ."

At this point Professor Peter Packer Pollinger began
blowing through his mustache, always a sign, as Kate well
knew, that he was about to burst into speech. Professor
Pollinger had only three kinds of speeches. The first was
about punctuation, particularly about the necessity of
keeping all punctuation marks *inside* quotation marks.
He had been known to go on about the unbelievable dan-
gers involved in placing punctuation marks *outside* quotation marks for close on to two hours. His second speech
had to do with Fiona Macleod, the alter ego and pseudo-
nym of a turn-of-the-century Irish author named William
Sharp. He had managed (William Sharp, not Professor
Pollinger, although the confusion did appear to be in
some mysterious way appropriate) to get himself so
perfectly, so schizophrenically divided between himself
and his pseudonymous alter ego (who was, of course, a
lady) that he had been known to fall down in a fit if
William Sharp and his wife were invited to a dinner party
and Fiona Macleod overlooked. Professor Pollinger had
for the last ten years devoted himself (he was now sixty-
seven) to the collection of every possible datum about
William Sharp, and he was delighted, not to say compelled, to transmit whatever he had most recently learned
to anyone he encountered. Thus despite a good deal of
dodging behind doorways, everyone in the English
Department, but particularly the secretaries, who, being
rooted behind their desks, were less able to disappear,
became authorities on the life and times of William
Sharp/Fiona Macleod.

Professor Pollinger also had a third speech, which was
unassigned: variable, as the mathematicians say. This
speech might happen to do with any experience Professor
Pollinger had recently undergone which had sufficiently
caught his attention to be memorable: how a snow drift

into which he had absentmindedly walked had over-
whelmed him; the way he had heard the sound of the
Irish Sea quite clearly in his ears for a solid hour before
his wife returned to discover that the tub in the adjoining
bathroom had overflowed, leaving Professor Pollinger
ankle-deep in water; or, very occasionally, when truly
impelled by circumstances, Professor Pollinger would
deliver himself of a pertinent fact, which was always, as it
was now, alarmingly germane to the discussion.

"Auden was interested in engineering," Professor Pollinger now announced, blowing through his mustache.
"Wanted to be one. When the Oriental languages fellow
dropped out, I suggested an engineer." Professor Pollinger puffed for a moment or two. "Glad to discover they
had a Chinese engineer," he said. "That made it all right,
I thought. Couldn't find you," he added, looking sulkily
at Kate.

Kate coughed. "Then," she said, turning to the gentleman from Engineering, "your name isn't Professor
Chang?"

"Is," that gentleman insisted. "Contradiction, please.
Is."

"I see," said Kate, who didn't. "Well, then, perhaps we
can begin. Will you, Professor Pollinger, ask the usual first
question?"

"Certainly," said Professor Pollinger, puffing through
his mustache. "What made you choose this topic, Mr.
Whateveryournameis?"

"Please, Professor Pollinger," Kate said, "if you don't
mind, don't ask the question until we get the candidate
into the room."

"Very well," Professor Pollinger said crossly. "Very
well." Kate, going to the door to summon Mr. Cornford,
gave Professor Pollinger a baleful look. She seriously suspected him of putting them all on. Due to retire at the

end of this year, he found it suited his peculiar sense of humor to appear gaga, but Kate suspected that a delight in confusion allied with a general resentment of the modern world was chiefly responsible for his eccentric ways. He had, of course, not really directed this or any other dissertation, although he did read right through all of them searching for punctuation outside quotation marks.

"Please be seated, Mr. Cornford," Kate said. The committee, as was customary, arose at the entrance of the candidate. "We will now begin. Professor Pollinger, will you please ask the first question?"

"Mr., er, Whateveryournameis," puff-puff through the mustache, "do you happen to know if Auden ever read the poetic dramas of Fiona Macleod?"

"Perhaps," Kate interjected, "Mr. Cornford could begin by telling us why he chose . . ."

"Tell me please," Professor Chang said, turning courteously in his chair, "in China your Mr. Auden found limestone landscapes? And what, please, is dildo?"

How they got through the subsequent two hours—for Professor Kruger was very interested in Auden's experiences in Germany, and Professor Chang in everything—Kate never properly knew. But such a good time was had by all that they quite happily voted Mr. Cornford a distinction (which he thoroughly deserved) and Kate was still congratulating him when the other three had bowed themselves from the room.

"My God," Mr. Cornford said. "No one will ever believe it. Can it possibly be official? I shall go to my death, which I hope is far distant, telling the story of this examination, and no one, no one on God's green earth will ever, ever believe it. And this is the world of scholarship I want to enter."

Kate laughed. "Well, according to T. S. Eliot, Auden is no scholar, you know."

"Eliot liked his poetry."

"Of course he did. But he insisted Auden was no scholar all the same. Somebody asked why, and Eliot said: 'I was reading an introduction by him to a selection of Tennyson's poems, in which he said that Tennyson is the stupidest poet in the language. Now if Auden had been a scholar he would have been able to think of some stupider poets.' And if you, Mr. Cornford, had been around this university as long as I, you would know that it is better that a farcical examination produce a first-rate piece of work like yours than that a brilliantly run examination produce, as I have often seen it do, a farce."

"So Auden was right," Mr. Cornford said. " 'Against odds, methods of dry farming may produce grain.' But, oh my Lord. 'Your Mr. Auden, he found limestone landscapes in China?' " he mimicked.

Kate parted from Mr. Cornford at the door of the building; he was due to make a midnight plane. This, she thought, has been a day. But it has had its moments, she thought, chuckling to herself over Professor Chang, bless his heart.

"Going my way, lady?" a voice said. "Or, more exactly, may I be allowed to go yours?" With something of a flourish, a man who had clearly been waiting for her removed his beret and bowed. "Bill McQuire is the name," he said. "Remember me? Department of Economics. Statistics is my specialty. I advised you once that some figures you wanted to juggle could not reveal anything meaningful, being self-selected."

"I'm going to get a taxi," Kate said. "Can I drop you somewhere?"

"I wanted to talk with you," McQuire said, "on a quite impersonal matter. May I buy you a drink?"

"Can it be as important as all that? I've had a day."

"Very important. Dean Frogmore has been trying to reach you all day, but your telephone never answers. I've been delegated to drop round and catch you after your examination. Successful candidate, I hope?"

"Beyond my wildest expectations," Kate answered. "What's this all about?"

"I realize," McQuire said, "that I am perhaps not the ideal man to approach you. But when Frogmore asked, I had to say I was acquainted with you. Do you know of Boulding?"

"He isn't by any chance a character in a novel by Bulwer-Lytton or a citizen of an Emerging African Nation?"

"He's an economist, and he announced one of the great laws of modern times: if it exists, it must be possible. That's what I want to see you about: something which exists, but which everyone is saying is impossible."

"I have always thought," Kate said, "that you scientists and social scientists ought to emblazon on your walls a quotation from J. B. S. Haldane: 'How do you know that the planet Mars isn't carried around by an angel?' Will it express my utter confidence in your knightly qualities if I ask you up for a drink?"

"It will," Bill McQuire said, hailing a taxi. "Same place?"

"Same place," Kate said. "And who in hell is Dean Frogmore?"

Kate had consulted Bill McQuire some five years earlier, when the Admissions Office of the Graduate Faculties had co-opted her onto a committee to study the old patterns of admission and to evolve new ones. For the first time in her life Kate found herself confronted with statistics, with no knowledge what to do with them but a distinct sense that either the statistics before her or the conclusions to be drawn from them were faulty. Someone had suggested that she consult a statistician, and had suggested Bill McQuire. Professor McQuire had himself soon provided a new statistic in Kate's life. He was the only man she had

ever gone to bed with on the basis of a ten-hour acquaint-
ance, liked moderately well, and never, to all intents and
purposes, seen again.

They had, of course, met from time to time on University occasions, in the Faculty Club, once on a dissertation
committee when a student of Kate's had written on some
abstruse topic concerning economics and literature. They
greeted each other on these occasions not only with the
pleasant formality their surroundings required, but with
the pleasant indifference they both genuinely felt.

Now, when they had reached home, Kate left McQuire
in the living room to fix himself a drink. It was, Kate
thought, a room Auden would have approved of:

> *Spotless rooms*
> *where nothing's left lying about*
> *chill me, so do cups used for ashtrays or smeared*
> *with lipstick: the homes I warm to,*
> *though seldom wealthy, always convey a feeling*
> *of bills being promptly settled*
> *with checks that don't bounce.*

McQuire seemed to agree, for he was happily stretched out
in her Knoll chair when she returned. "It is extraordinarily
ungallant of me to say so," he laughed, "but when I
opened your liquor cabinet I had a most magnificent case
of *déja vû*. I remembered looking into it, years ago, whenever it was, and thinking: My God, Jack Daniel's, and
that's exactly what I did tonight. What can I get you?"

Kate asked for Scotch. She watched him as he fixed the
drink. How old was he now, somewhere between forty-
five and fifty? His curly hair was thinner, and gray; at least
he doesn't dye it, Kate thought, and was surprised to have
thought it. Bill had always worn his curly hair longer than
the prevailing style—he was a distinctly Byronic type—
and now that fashions had overtaken him he looked oddly

more out of style than he had previously done. His face was lined, with that special crinkled quality of the skin which marks those who have drunk heavily and long. Turning to her with the drink, he found himself held by her stare. "Portrait of an aging stag," he said. "Dissipated but kindly. If you want to know the whole hideous truth, I like them younger and younger all the time, so that I am in danger of becoming a dirty old man. Humbert Humbert, I do pity thee. Well, no," he added, seeing Kate's eyes widen. "Eighteen is still my under limit. Cheers."

"I am trying to decide," Kate said, "why it is that you are quite incapable of shocking me, even though I think your life reprehensible and I find promiscuity shocking, particularly in married men."

"I'm sure you do. In fact, I have often noticed that those most shocked by marital infidelity are usually themselves unmarried. Cecelia, as it happens, has settled quite nicely into life, though she is pleased to see that neither of our sons at all resembles a rampant stag—that is, me. *You've* worn well, Kate. I like you and the way you look, and you're very decent to put up with me this afternoon."

"I haven't worn all that well. Supposedly I shall always be tall and lean with a French twist and a face that shows all the worries in the world. Do you know what I like about you, Bill? It's only just occurred to me, so let me say it and then we can get down to whatever you and Dean Toadwell have on your minds."

"His name is Frogmore. What do you like? My eternal evanescence?"

"The fact that however much you stalk your prey, you do not class women with motor cars if they are attractive and with eye-flies if they are not."

"Eye-flies?"

"Well, something nasty. I was quoting Forster, who

happened to be writing about India at the time, so it was eye-flies."

"Somebody said once—unlike you I never remember where I read things—that if a woman is not beautiful at twenty, it's not her fault; if she's not beautiful at forty, it is her fault. Have you ever thought of getting married?"

"Once or twice, lately. The ramifications of university upheavals are endless. Do you think marriage advisable? One has such lovely friendships with men whose wives were beautiful when they were twenty."

"What a dreadfully cynical remark. Married women can have friends; the men feel, if anything, more comfortable."

"Meaning you would feel more comfortable now if I were married."

"Kate, don't put words in my mouth. I was . . ."

"Answer me honestly, if you want me to help with your beastly crisis."

"That's not fair. People who demand to be answered honestly have already decided what the honest answer is. But you'd be wrong. I wouldn't be more comfortable with you, but I think I would feel you were happier, particularly in these times of institutionalized uncertainty."

"I'll tell you one thing, Bill," Kate said, recovering herself. "I have believed, in the words of a first-rate woman scholar who lived to be eighty and was always falling in love with someone, that marriage for a woman spoils the two things that make life glorious: learning and friendship. Somehow, that no longer seems so unquestionably true. Fill up your glass and tell me about Toadwell."

"Frogmore. That you haven't heard of him is absolutely symptomatic."

"Oh, come on, Bill, how many deans have I heard of?"

"Can you name the Dean of Divinity? Law, Graduate Faculties, Public Administration, Business, Engineering?"

"Not Public Administration."

"My point still holds."

"I can only name most of the others because of the troubles last spring."

"Fair enough. But you can't name the Dean of the University College?"

"Frogmore?"

"Frogmore."

"You know, Bill, it is absolutely coming over me in waves that I do not *want* to know the Dean of the University College, or University College, or . . ."

"Shall I tell you something? Last spring, when this place was blowing up, there was only one school in it that remained intact."

"Don't tell me, let me guess."

"The students of the University College occupied their own building and held it for themselves. They proved to be the only really loyal student body the whole blasted University possessed, and the University, with the gratitude and intelligence that has marked all its decisions, now wants to wash the University College down the drain."

"Bill, I'm in Graduate Faculties. I'm planning next year's curriculum there. I'm going to give a text course in the novels of Bulwer-Lytton, and maybe one in the literature of Emerging African Nations. I'm thinking of emigrating to an Emerging African Nation myself. Do you really think you want to try to make this my problem?"

"Yes, lady, I do. And when your fortieth birthday comes, I shall buy you a specially lovely present for a beautiful and humane woman."

"As Polly Spence would say—my God, Polly Spence— four-letter-word-bathroom. Bull's, that is."

CHAPTER
TWO

In our morale must lie our strength.

"All I ask, Kate, is that you listen. Give it a chance. Try to remember that these are people fighting for the life of a school *they* do not need. They all have tenure in other branches of the University. It's a matter of believing in something."

"Even Dean Frogmore?"

"Even he." Bill McQuire and Kate were walking toward the Faculty Club next day to attend a luncheon with Dean Frogmore and some senior members of his faculty. Kate had had to cancel two appointments to come, and she did so, finally, only as a favor to McQuire. He had known, and Kate respected him for knowing, that she had learned to refuse any official request, but was still far from immune to personal ones. "Frogmore is offered a job every other day, as president of this college or that. Everyone's looking for administrators; they're almost as scarce as plumbers and doctors. Probably he'll go off to some rural collegiate paradise before long, but I think his devotion to the University College is unquestionable. Everyone has underestimated Frogmore from the beginning, I among them. But let me tell you two things about him: he's got guts you'll admire, and an oily surface you'll hate. For one thing, and I want to warn you about this in advance, knowing your prejudices, he calls everyone, *everyone*, by his first name the first moment they meet."

"Cripes," Kate said.

"I know; that's why I mention it. You're remarkably old-world in some ways, Kate."

"Remarkably. I don't mind going to bed at ten at night with a man I met at noon the same day, but I can't bear being called by my first name until a relationship has had time to mature. Very old-world indeed."

McQuire chuckled. "It's a maddening habit—Frogmore's, I mean. When I first met him he kept referring to Lou and Teddy, and the conversation had gone on for half an hour before I realized he was speaking of the President and Vice-President of the University. But don't underestimate him, Kate. He really and truly wants to put the University College on the map, when the easiest thing for him to do would be to cop out."

"It might be the easiest thing for all of us. Certainly for me. I can't imagine, truthfully, why you think I . . ."

"Yes, you can. Be good now. I'll give you a chance later to protest and thrash around, and I promise you, if your answer is really 'No,' I'll back you up."

"Which means if I act intelligently interested today, and ask leading questions, you won't assume I'm committed."

"Have I told you yet today," Bill said, "that you're beautiful?"

The luncheon party was held in one of the private rooms of the Faculty Club. The moment Kate and Bill McQuire entered, Frogmore leaped to his feet and rushed forward to greet them at the door. Somewhat overcome by his enthusiasm, the other gentlemen already seated around the table rose to their feet, awkwardly pushing back their chairs, dropping their napkins and brushing crumbs from their laps. (It was one of the unfailing characteristics of the Faculty Club that although service never began until the latest possible moment after one had sat down, there was always present, as part of the table setting, a large, exceedingly stale roll which one found oneself compelled, in time, to pulverize, showering oneself and the table top with crumbs.)

"Please," Kate weakly said. The academic community had taken longer than most to shake off old habits of gallantry. When Kate had first joined the faculty she had had to become inured to roomfuls of men rising to their feet as she entered. Gradually, of course, the custom had died out. Only Frogmore, with his bouncy manner and boy-scout demeanor, had trapped them into old habits.

"So this is Kate," Frogmore said. "Thank you, Bill, for bringing her." Kate, regarding Frogmore with a lackluster eye, avoided glancing at McQuire. Clever he: the blow fell less painfully, being expected. "Let me introduce you pronto to the others before getting under way; we've got a long agenda. What will you drink, Kate? This is on me; the Dean's slush fund."

"A Bloody Mary please," Kate demurely said. (Reed had often remarked that when Kate came all over demure, it meant that what she really wanted to do was put a pillow over some chap's head and sit on it.) Kate did not like, in the ordinary way, to drink at lunch, a meal she avoided if she could, and certainly not when she was in danger of becoming involved in some internecine struggle. She had therefore hit upon the lovely stratagem of ordering a drink which was, at the Faculty Club, equal parts of Worcestershire sauce and watery tomato juice with as little vodka as made no difference to anyone not a teetotaler on principle.

"You know everybody, I'm sure," Frogmore said. "Luther Hankster of Biology." Kate, indeed, had stood side by side with Luther Hankster when the police had first and, as it turned out, abortively, been called to clear out the administration building. Playboy turned radical, Hankster kept more or less in the good graces of his colleagues by his unerring good manners and the careful use of a voice never, ever, raised. He was given to outrageously radical pronouncements which, had they been delivered in any but the voice of a man making secret love, would have instantly offended everyone.

"George Castleman, of course, is our guiding star." Kate wanted to ask Castleman if he had been tempted lately to public disrobement, but contained herself; she wondered anew at the passion for clichés which seemed, in Frogmore's case, almost to equal his passion for first names. Castleman, if not a guiding star, was certainly a power in the University, on all the vital committees and possessed of the kind of political acumen that was almost as rare in an academic community as inspired teaching.

"Herbert Klein, Political Science. Herbie, I believe you're not as well known to Kate as the rest of us." "Herbie," a man of enormous dignity and baleful looks, rose and shook Kate's hand with a firmness clearly indicating his wish to dissociate both of them from Frogmore's unearned intimacy. Kate wondered if anyone else had ever called him Herbie in his life. "We hope you will be able to help us, Professor Fansler," he formally said. Kate suppressed a grin.

"And," Frogmore went relentlessly on, "this is the other stranger to you, Kate: John Peabody, a student in the University College."

"Hi," said Peabody, to whom formality was unknown. Kate looked up in surprise. Although the principle of students serving on all the governing bodies of the University had by now been given token acceptance, in fact where there was a need for delicate decisions, students had so far not usually been present. Peabody, though, was older than any ordinary college man: he looked nearer thirty than twenty.

"And Tony Cartier is of course from your own department." Kate could never resist smiling at the sight of Cartier: his ill-controlled restlessness made luncheon meetings a torture to him; he would glance wildly about as though at any moment someone might lock the doors and keep him prisoner here forever.

The aged waiter took the order for the drinks and scrutinized it with exaggerated care. All the waiters at the Faculty Club were old and slow, though those chosen for the private rooms were, if not fast, because that was clearly impossible, at least not deliberately slower than age and rheumatism determined. Finding, perhaps to his sorrow, no esoteric and therefore unavailable drinks on the list, the waiter departed.

Frogmore began to speak. He had not spoken long before Kate became aware that he was, for all his foolish ways, a genius at committee work. Kate, who thought herself remarkably inept on committees, recognized the talent instantly. Thank God, Kate thought; were Frogmore a bumbler they would all be wasting their patience and their time.

"Now," Frogmore said, "let us run over the major points in a swift recapitulation, mostly for your benefit, Kate, since the rest of us have been kicking this thing around for quite a while. I don't want to be long-winded, so I'll get down to the nitty-gritty, the nuts and bolts." (Kate had, by the end of this sentence, ceased even to wince; she was taking her beating manfully. "There is one evil which . . . should never be passed over in silence but be continually publicly attacked, and that is corruption of the language . . ." Auden had written, but then Auden's hours were not passed amidst deans and social scientists.)

"As you know, Kate," Frogmore went blissfully on, "the University, which used to be a collection of baronies, has got to start operating as a whole if it's not to be part of the state system in ten years. There are certain changes we all agree on: it would take three million dollars to make our Dental School adequate; ten million to make it outstanding. Do we really need a Dental School? No, we do not. But, you see, restructuring is a convenient excuse for carrying out long-planned hanky-panky. I take it you are familiar with Professor Jeremiah Cudlipp?" Kate, who knew a rhetorical question when she heard one, did not trouble either to nod or object. "He, of course, and his associate, Bob O'Toole, have decided that this time of restructuring is just the moment to bounce the University College off the campus altogether."

"Bounce it?"

"Demolish it, phase it out, declare it null and void, give it the ax."

"But Cudlipp is only Chairman of the College English Department," Kate said.

"There is no 'only' about it, I'm afraid," Castleman said. "For reasons we do not wholly understand, he is determined that the University College must go. It gives a bachelor's degree that Cudlipp claims dilutes the prestige of the degree given by *The* College, as they so maddeningly call it. He has lots of other arguments. The point is, since he is in the English Department, we felt we needed someone in addition to Professor Cartier to help us in what is, I'm afraid, a fight for survival."

"The College feels," Luther Hankster whispered, "like someone with valuable suburban property whose neighbor threatens to sell to a black."

"Does Bob O'Toole go along with this? I have always thought of him as a follower of Clemance."

"So he is," Castleman said. "But, as perhaps you have noticed, he possesses arrogance and ambition in about equally large proportions, which puts him squarely on Cudlipp's side."

"Where does Clemance stand?"

"Oh," McQuire said, "he's with the College; always has been. He suggests, in his marvelously reasonable way, that we are simply not 'excellent' enough. Which is nonsense; we are the most excellent college for adults in the country."

"Have you had much to do with the College, Professor Fansler?" Herbert Klein asked.

"Enough to know they are in danger of giving arrogance a bad name," Kate lightly said.

"Exactly," Frogmore exclaimed, clapping his hands together. "Well put, Kate."

"O.K.," Kate said. "You want someone from the English Department—which you gather, correctly, is fed up with Cudlipp's throwing all that weight around." She hoped Frogmore would consider that well put too.

"And," Castleman said, "we need general sort of help so that when the Administrative Council next meets they will confirm the future of the University College in no uncertain terms. Needless to say, Cudlipp will do all he can to prevent that."

"Right," Kate said. "I see, or think I do. But why me? I don't even like teaching undergraduates."

"You are more decorative than our other colleagues," Cartier said.

"We did a lot of research, Kate," Frogmore said, "and we ran into very little flak when it came to you." (My God, Kate thought, he *is* smart; smart enough to know the we-chose-you-for-your-womanly-charms bit wouldn't work; good for him.) "From all sides we heard of your sympathy with students—your willingness, long before the roof fell in, to give them time. We also heard that you are opposed to the publish-or-perish racket, and to professors who have no time for anything but their own professional careers."

"All exaggerated, I assure you. I have no recent experience in undergraduate teaching and, to be brutally frank, not much desire for it. I like graduate students because they're self-selected." She winked at Bill McQuire.

"Why do you dislike teaching undergraduates?" Hankster asked. "Or did you just say that to startle us?"

"I said it because it's true—and tact isn't my most notable characteristic. Why is it true? Because of the age of undergraduates—delightful, no doubt, but not for me. As far as I'm concerned, youth is a condition which will pass, and which I prefer to have pass outside of my immediate field of vision. Of course, I have nothing *against* young people—apart from the fact that they are arrogant, spoiled, discourteous, incapable of compromise, and unaware of the price of everything they want to destroy. It's not that I disagree with their beliefs, or mind if I do disagree. I just prefer those whom life has had time to season.

"What a long speech. I am certain I ought not to be so emphatic; for one thing, it's unladylike and mysteriously unbecoming not to cherish the company of the young of one's own species. Someone must have asked me a question, and now I've come all over nasty about children, and quite forgotten what it was."

"We are answering the question of why you were chosen to join us," Klein said. "We felt we could interest you in a college whose students are no longer in the throes of role-playing: older, experienced in the ways of the world, mellower on the whole, and totally motivated—self-selected was, I believe, your own phrase."

"I see," Kate said. "And am I to be persuaded to some special action, or only encouraged to cheer in a general sort of way?"

"Let some of our students into your courses," Frogmore said. "Get to know them. Find out a bit about what we're doing, and give us a chance to impress you. Carry our banner in the Graduate English Department any way you see fit, but fight our cause there."

"I've certainly no objection to a few of your students in my courses, if I can interview them first. As to the fight in the Graduate English Department—you know, I don't as a

35

rule drink at lunch, but right at the moment I feel the need of what Auden calls an 'analeptic swig.'"

.   .   .

"You've got to admit, Reed, it's not madly *me*. I mean, can you imagine *one* getting involved in a university power-struggle?"

"Then don't," Reed said. "What I can't imagine is why you don't just say no, but then I, like all outsiders, am having a certain amount of trouble understanding what in the world is going on in that university of yours. Surely you can send this Frogmore chap a firm but gracious note telling him you don't want anything to do with his silly college."

"But am I certain I don't want anything to do with it? It is, after all, awfully soul-satisfying of them to want me."

"And a very clever bunch they are, I must say. Though it is certainly by no means clear to me why the proposition of any old college gets the most careful consideration, while my . . ."

"I have yet to refuse one of your propositions, Reed, admit it."

"Kate, whenever you start talking like a bad imitation of Nancy Mitford I know that you are not only plastered but worried."

"Sweet, perceptive you. Though I must say, I really can't believe that Auden drank a whole bottle of Cherry Heering." They were in Kate's living room late that night and Kate, as she carefully explained, while she had long since admitted she couldn't write poetry like Auden's, wanted to discover if she had at least his capacity for alcohol. "You see," she had told Reed, "Auden went to spend the evening with the Stravinskys and Robert Craft, and he managed to drink a pitcher of martinis before dinner, a bottle of champagne during, and a bottle of Cherry Heering after. Craft thinks he thought the Cherry Heering was Chianti—I rather wish it were, actually. All that affected his labials only slightly and his wit not at all. It had no effect either, apparently, on his stomach, his liver, or his plumbing—not one visit to the loo. Well, I have failed the test—that is, my stomach is all right; I have, thank God, no way of knowing *how* my liver is; I'm far too comfortable to go to the loo; but I am not going to make it through this bottle of Cherry Heering. To join the fight or not to join the fight, that is the question. Whether it is nobler in the mind to defeat Jeremiah Cudlipp, which would be so pleasant in the gut, to say nothing of the good one could do, or . . ."

"Kate," Reed said, "what has happened to you this fall? Last spring, at least before all those students decided to occupy all those buildings, you seemed to . . ."

"Sara Teasdale."

"I beg your pardon?"

> *In the spring I asked the daisies*
> *If his words were true,*
> *And the clever little daisies*
> *Always knew.*
>
> *Now the fields are brown and barren,*
> *Bitter autumn blows,*
> *And of all the stupid asters*
> *Not one knows.*"

"I am certain," Reed said, "that Auden does not quote Sara Teasdale even after three bottles of Cherry Heering. What are you worried about, this University College?"

"There is my motto."

"Oh, my God, which motto is that? If a thing is worth doing, it's worth doing badly?"

"Not that one. The British Navy one: never ask for a job, never refuse one."

"I wonder if I, too, am not an honorary member of the British Navy: I'm thinking of leaving the D.A.'s Office."

"Reed Amhearst! Why? Surely you haven't tired of fighting crime?"

"I've been offered a job—actually a partnership—in a Wall Street law firm. Great rise in salary, among other things. A man might even consider supporting a wife and a small canary."

"Do you mean you would help people merge companies and diddle with their stocks and bonds?"

"No. That's what everyone else in the firm does. I would be expected to rally round when their clients take time off and start diddling with things *other* than stocks and bonds. I am distressed, Kate, that the more certain I become of what I want, the more uncertain you become. I do realize that the University has got to go through a time of reorganization and re-examination, but—well, you seem positively driven . . ."

"To get plastered."

"Yes, but I was going to say—to examine every alternative as though you had somehow forfeited the right to say a simple 'no' to anything."

"But I have, you know. In former days, everyone found the assumption of innocence so easy; today we find fatally easy the assumption of guilt. The generation gap appeared somewhere between me and my brothers. They deny that they are guilty of anything but an excess of generosity, and I deny that I am innocent in anything except bumbling good intentions. Excuse me a minute, I think I'm going to throw up."

Reed, watching her more or less dignified exit, decided this was hyperbole. She returned, indeed, in a cheerful mood.

"I have thought it all out," Kate said. "Ready? The University College is a damn good idea, and there is nothing against it except the insufferable snobbery of the College. The fact is, now that I come to think of it, I know plenty of people of my generation of all sexes to whom an adult college of excellence would be the chance for a new life or a second life, which is becoming more and more necessary in the United States but which present institutions make impossible. Hooray, I'm going to make a speech. Ladies and gentlemen . . ."

"Right," Reed said. "Then drop Frogmore a short, gracious note saying let's fight together shoulder to shoulder for good old University College, sincerely yours, Kate Fansler."

"Just Kate. He never uses last names."

"Good. Then you join the fight for University, and I'll join my law firm. Why not?"

"Frederick Clemance."

"Our hero."

"You need not be vulgar. When you speak with admiration of all those musty forensic types, I do not sneer."

"I'm not sneering, simply surprised to have his name introduced into the discussion. What's he got to do with University College?"

"He's against it. Lock, stock, and barrel—or do I mean hook, line, and sinker? Anyway, he hates it, he wants to crush it under foot, he has joined with Jeremiah Cudlipp to defeat it, and do I want to go into battle with those two?"

"Why not? Growing up consists in fighting our former heroes."

"Maybe. I'm not that grown up. I don't want to get close enough to Clemance to discover he's not as great as I prefer to suppose he is."

"I don't know about the labials but the sibilants are doing fine. If I remember correctly Auden's poem on the death of Yeats, which isn't all that difficult since you cannot have read it to me fewer than eighteen times, Auden found no difficulty in recognizing that Yeats was magnificent and silly at the same time. Something about time forgiving those who wrote well. Clemance, if I am to believe you, wrote well. Let time forgive him, and get on with your college."

"But Clemance isn't silly; he's always been large of soul when all about him were nit-picking. Anyway, I've been hero-worshipping him since before I got into his special seminar as a student, and that, God help me, was nearly twenty years ago."

"If Clemance is as large-souled as all that, why does he associate himself with Jeremiah Cudlipp?"

"I don't know. Love for the College, maybe."

"Maybe."

Kate got to her feet and wandered over to the bookcase. Clemance's books were there, ranged together, biographies, essays, plays, poems—all together, a rare tribute in itself, since Kate divided her library ruthlessly into categories: poetry, fiction, drama, biography, criticism, cultural history, and books-not-worth-keeping-with-which-I-cannot-bear-to-part. "And if this were a movie," Reed said, "we would flash back to eager young Kate, eyes shining, hair streaming down her back, listening to Clemance in the glory of his prime, explaining us to ourselves."

"My hair never streamed down my back, surely it's the prime of his glory, and I wish they still made movies like that."

"He must be almost as old as Auden."

"We're all almost as old as Auden, 'in middle-age hoping to twig from/What we are not what we might be next.'"

"I'll tell you what you and Clemance are going to be next."

"What?"

"On opposite sides. Do you think I could be present at the opening fusilades of what promises to be a most interesting skirmish?"

"You can if you want to join us tomorrow. Frederick

Clemance, though you may not believe it, has invited me to lunch. Why should you want to support a small canary?"

"Why should I want to support a wife? The only woman I think of marrying has long supported herself, with the aid of a meager salary and a large private income, and is presently concerned with founding a new college."

"I'm not founding a college, I'm allocating resources— that is, if you're describing me. Are you thinking of marrying me for my money?"

"Odd you should mention that," Reed said. "It's the only reason for marrying you I hadn't thought of. Now, when it comes to the reasons for *not* marrying you, there isn't an argument I've missed. But I'm like the Jew in Boccaccio who was converted to Catholicism on the sensible grounds that if the Church has succeeded despite all the corruption he found in Rome, it must have God behind it."

"The world is full of beautiful young women aching for a handsome man like you, all graying sideburns and youthful demeanor. I am aging, cantankerous, given to illogical skirmishes and the drinking of too much wine. There must be at least fifty young women waiting for you, Reed."

Reed walked then, in his turn, to the bookcase (poetry), extracted a volume and read from it: " 'One deed ascribed to Hercules was "making love" with fifty virgins in the course of a single night: one might on that account say that Hercules was beloved of Aphrodite, but one would not call him a lover.' Nor is that all," Reed said, turning the pages. "We have all agreed we live in uncertain times. Indeed, says Auden:

'How much half-witted horseplay and sheer bloody
    misrule
It took to bring you two together both on schedule?' "

CHAPTER THREE

If equal affection cannot be,
Let the more loving one be me.

Saturday morning, and Central Park free for human beings to move at the speeds they might have attained at the turn of the century: horses, bicycles, and the almost forgotten pleasures of walking. Kate and Reed, whenever they considered the incredible series of disasters to which living in New York City regularly exposed one—strikes, garbage uncollected, snow unremoved, no transportation, no heat, no safety in the streets—or whenever they heard others complain of city living, would always think: they have taken the automobiles out of Central Park on weekends. It was the one urban blessing the decade had conferred.

"To return," Reed said, "to the conversation of last night, why has misrule and horseplay brought you to such a state of discombobulation? Or, since it has, may I offer my help in recombobulation? Does the University matter that much?"

"On Thursday, when the semester began," Kate said, "I asked myself that question—not, perhaps, whether it matters, which it so clearly does, but why?" Kate stopped to pat a puppy who came loping up anticipating admiration. "I can remember many stages of the revolution or insurrection or whatever it might be called. The exhilaration of the week when the buildings were occupied, the sense of absolute aliveness which, despite all the problems, one did so ringingly feel. I remember being shoved against a building by a plainclothesman with a club and thinking, this is it. I remember hearing the endlessly repeated obscenities from the students who stood about on the ledges and roofs of the buildings like acroterium, and wondering if indeed, as one of the characters in one of Forster's novels notes, they were out of fashion. I remember watching the flowers and grass being trampled, distinctly noticing as the last tulip was crushed. I remember, on the first day when they occupied the President's Office, walking by the administration building and thinking: so that's where the President's Office is, and never wondering, then, why in all the years I had been associated with the University I had never learned where the President's Office was, nor cared to learn. Later on, of course, we heard that the guards had entered the office, not to try to bounce the students but to rescue a Van Gogh which hung there, and I did muse then to think that I had never known the University possessed one of the world's great paintings.

"But none of that was the worst, you know; it only seemed the worst to those on the outside, who were appalled at the actions of the students, or appalled at the actions of the police—when what I became so suddenly struck with was the fact that there had never really *been* a university. That a bunch of half-baked, foul-mouthed Maoist students could bring a great university to a standstill, could be followed in their illegal acts by nearly a thousand moderate, thoughtful students, but above all could reveal that the University had never really been administered at all. We had a president whom no one ever saw, whose understanding of the true condition of the University could not have been more inaccurate if his job had been running a yacht club in East Hampton; we had a Board of Governors who had never, literally never, spoken to a student nor visited the University except for the monthly meetings, when their chauffeurs drove them to the campus; we had a faculty so busy with its own affairs that it had not troubled to observe that there was no university, only separate egos, departments, schools, programs all staking claims.

"Do you know, Reed, my brothers, who needless to say were outraged to the last degree that a bunch of unwashed radicals could be allowed to wield such powers, could never understand that there was any fault at work but that of the students and perhaps their overindulgent parents. They could not understand that a fumbling, withdrawn administration and a self-indulged, indifferent faculty were as much to blame as a youthful generation's failure to observe 'law and order.' There were students in those buildings, students I had known in class, who were no more Maoist than I was, who said that the communal life inside the buildings was the first vital experience they had had since they entered the University. We let it all go dead on us, Reed. Whatever may have happened in other universities, whatever may have been the destructive glee of radical groups at other places—Berkeley, Columbia, or wherever—the blame for what happened to my university was mine—mine and my associates."

"Those kids were an outrageous group—the radical core."

"They were. But to blame them for everything that followed is to blame the First World War on the assassin at Sarajevo. I am not, of course, very good at historical analogies. Auden says that:

> at any hour from some point else
> May come another tribal outcry
> Of a new generation of birds who chirp
> Not for effect but because chirping
>
> Is the thing to do.

I know all that; I know it is true of student rebellions at other universities now. But not of my university."

"Are you going ahead with the University College crusade then in an attempt to grab some stones from the wreckage and build them into a more lasting edifice?"

"Sorry if I've been going on. All the same, it does intrigue me that the University College was the single unit in the University where the students, faculty, and administration did not automatically, or even eventually, assume they were working at cross purposes. The faculty at *The* College went about either in open disgust or like fathers who have done everything for their sons only to be sneered at, treated with disdain and ingratitude. The graduate students revealed that they had long suffered agony from the outworn structures and grading systems of their schools. But Frogmore's little domain held off chaos and went on with its work. That interests me."

They stopped by the lake to watch the rowing. "Shall we rent a boat?" Reed asked. Kate shook her head.

"Sorry to run on so," she said. "I keep trying to put it all into place. All right, I want to say, we were wrong; O.K., we were wrong, we will rebuild. But what a job! All the easy relations of the faculty, one with the other, gone. People have each other tagged now: radical, conservative, untrustworthy. Reed, I wanted to ask you something."

"I know."

"You do? How do you know?"

"Talented me, from the District Attorney's Office. I've known you awhile, Kate. I always know when you have a speech ready, and I know that you do not proceed through martinis and champagne to Cherry Heering because Auden did. You couldn't make the speech sober or, we now know, drunk. How about on a lovely fall morning? Shall we rent bicycles?"

"You have suggested everything but horses. And I haven't ridden in—oh, since another lifetime. We could of course take one of those horse-drawn carriages."

"Shall we?"

"Let's walk. We can get a beer at the boathouse."

They got the beers, walking in silence, and took them to a spot on a hill where they could watch the bicyclists, most of them pushing the bikes but a few riding, straining to reach the top. Kate liked to watch the moment when those who had struggled up on their bicycles let the wind catch them, going down.

> *"We may someday need very much to*
> *Remember when we were happy.*

The life before last spring seems to have been a time of innocence. I am no longer certain of anything, Reed, but I think that in my uncertainty, I would like to live with you, if you will have me."

"Live with me. What does that mean?"

"Even words don't mean anything anymore. Live with you. Occupy the same premises, have the same address. Pretend to be married."

"Pretend?" Reed leaned against a tree, with his hands in his pockets. "The one word I never expected to hear you use. I've asked you to marry me often enough; I don't mind if you ask me."

"I don't believe in marriage; not at my age, anyway."

"Kate, what I cannot pretend is that this University turmoil has improved you. You've developed all sorts of alarming symptoms, not least of which is a constant reference to yourself as on the brink of total decrepitude. People get married at your age, as you very well know, and indeed at twice your age. At any rate, if you are doddering, I am doddering even more, and do not find myself in the slightest inspired, as you seem to expect me to be, by the thought of a wife twenty years my junior, however luscious she might be."

"Reed, I—even Auden wrote a *Dichtung und Wahreit*

about love, and not a love poem. There are no words for the words I want to say."

"May I suggest some? Simple, straightforward, unmistakable?"

"They would not be for what I want to say. I've funked it. Why the assurance of being me should be affected by the occupation of a President's Office which I would not, in any case, have been able even to find, I can't say. I don't know. Now, being a woman alone doesn't seem as easy as it has been. I need, for a time anyway, the sense of being part of a partnership; oh, I mean every petty thing you may wonder about: all the confidence of having a man. But none of that seems to me grounds for marriage."

"What a very odd idea of marriage you must have. The only people who could possibly have lived up to it were Tristan and Isolde, and all they could do was die. In fact, now I come to think of it, all great lovers cannot choose but die because marriage is essentially mundane and quotidian and useful."

" 'A game, like war, that calls for patience, foresight, maneuver, for those with their wander-years behind them,' Auden once said."

"He has said a good deal, I'll grant him that. Do you know what I think? I think you would have changed anyway, even if your university had not come falling down like London Bridge. It's simple enough; all we do is find a pig with a ring on the end of his nose, his nose, and get married."

"Reed, I do want a ring, from a pig or merely from Tiffany's, I want to be half of a pair, as though the world and every dinner party were Noah's ark and one could not attend except in pairs, but I don't want actually, legally to get married. I want you to be legally free."

Reed laughed. "You want a sham, a plain, unadorned sham, because you won't allow yourself to be someone's

47

wife, like any other proper woman. You can't share my
apartment unless you marry me, so there!"

"It seems to me shameful to turn to you now and say
let's get married because I now need a security I didn't in
the least mind scorning before. What I meant about all
the luscious young women is simply a recognition of the
fact that it is easier for men to marry."

"I am not 'men,' and I doubt that I should find it easy
at all to marry. Shall I tell you what worries you? No, don't
stop me. I've never known you to balk at the truth, and
you shan't now. From some new-found weakness, like one
recovering from an illness, you are seeking to belong—to
me, as it so fortunately happens. Not only does it seem
unfair to you to capitulate in weakness to what you
refused in strength, but you know that the love you have
for me is not of the same timbre, not even of the same
scale, as the love I have for you. Don't protest. I know it
makes little sense. I agree it makes little sense. I a handsome, talented, affable man in the prime of life, you an
aging, argumentative, irrational spinster. But sense or not,
I love you, and if we marry it shall be properly, with a
ring and a judge and a license so that if you decide to
leave me or I you I shall at least not be cheating some
lawyer out of the chance to arrange a divorce. Do your
brothers have to come to the wedding? I'm glad to hear
they don't, because frankly the thought of your brothers
terrifies me. Kate, let's get married on Thanksgiving.
That way, we don't have to remember the date even, we
can just celebrate on the last Thursday in every November
—which will be a holiday, so much more convenient if you
stop to think about it. Aren't you going to say something?"

"I was thinking," Kate said, "that I never really asked
the daisies, and they never told me, but this fall, all the
asters knew."

"I am willing enough to put up with Auden," Reed

said with lapidary phrasing, "I am even willing to quote a bit of Auden now and then on my own, but I want to make *quite* clear that I will not put up with the poetry of Sara Teasdale."

CHAPTER
FOUR

the funniest
mortals and the kindest are those who are most aware
of the baffle of being, don't kid themselves our care
is consolable, but believe a laugh is less
heartless than tears.

Kate had been astonished at Frederick Clemance's invitation to lunch. She felt as nervous, she told Reed, as a teenager on a first date. I mean, she tried to explain, I have worshipped him, or close to it, and what can we possibly find to say now, over an atrocious vegetable omelette at the Faculty Club. I know, Kate said, I am terrified, in Auden's words, of discovering that a god worth kneeling-to for a while has tabernacled and rested.

Yet her first thought, when she and Clemance were seated, was how old he looked. The spring occurrences had aged him. He had allowed his white hair to grow long, which became him, since he now resembled not so much Emerson as Kate's idea of Emerson. Yet it was not his white hair nor lined face nor sixty years which most distressed Kate, sitting opposite him, as his indefinable air of regret, perhaps even of despair.

"So it took a revolution for us to lunch together," he said. "That is too bad. Well, perhaps it is all destiny—I think, you know, the Greeks were right: family curses are easier to live with than personal failure."

"Oh, I'm not so sure," Kate said. "It must be aggravating

to find yourself in trouble 'because of a great-great-grandmother who got laid by a sacred beast.' "

Clemance smiled. "How *was* the Auden dissertation?" he asked. "I quite forgot, with all these goings-on. You were good to help me out."

Kate decided that the details of that particular event were perhaps best glossed over. "It was an excellent dissertation—it managed to appreciate Auden's poetry without patronizing him or his life. Mr. Cornford was blessed with the understanding that while a new poem of Auden's is an event in all *our* biographies, we have no business meddling with his."

"Wouldn't you like to meet him, all the same?"

"No," Kate said. "Not for a moment. Oh, I do rather hope one day to hear him read his poems, or catch him again on the telly. But meet him: no. I should be afraid of boring him to death; or worse, going on, like the juggins he mentions in the poem to MacNeice, who went on about Alienation. If I met him I would be certain to be so nervous I would go on about *something*. Besides, Auden's just a man: as full of demons and petty irritations and unkindnesses as the rest of us—he's bound to be. What I cherish are the poems, and the persona, the literary biography of him I've accumulated over the years."

"Your instincts are probably right. As Auden says in one of his small humorous poems: 'I have no gun, but I can spit.' What are the main events you've accumulated in the biography of Auden's persona?"

Kate looked at Clemance. She admired enormously his attempts at lightness. Kate found herself thinking of Auden's poem to T. S. Eliot:

It was you who, not speechless from shock but finding
the right
language for thirst and fear, did much
to prevent a panic.

"Well," she said, "what I have is a series of snapshots, really, caught by Auden's friends. Isherwood describing Auden's hats: the opera hat, 'belonging to the period when he decided that poets ought to dress like bank directors, in morning cutaways and striped trousers or evening swallowtails. There was a workman's cap, with a shiny black peak, which he bought while he was living in Berlin, and which had, in the end, to be burnt, because he was sick into it one evening in a cinema.' There was a Panama with a black ribbon, representing Auden's 'conception of himself as a lunatic clergyman; always a favorite role.' Isherwood is really the richest source of Auden lore. My favorite of all is Auden in China in 1938 listening with Isherwood to the translation of a poem written in their honor in Chinese. Not to be outdone, Auden replied with a sonnet he had finished writing the day before. Auden had a visiting card in China with his name on it: *Mr. Au Dung*." Kate chuckled. "There's much more, but, of course, you know him, so it seems . . ."

"Do, please, go on," Clemance said.

"Some of Auden's anecdotes are unprintable, though of course I've seen them in print. I especially appreciate the critic who said of Auden that he is able to write prolifically, carelessly, and exquisitely without seeming to have to pay any price for his inspiration. He is the only poet I know of whom that is true—good poet, that is."

"I thought you didn't read critics on Auden."

"I don't; coming on that was just a bit of serendipity."

"Do you know Auden's explanation for today's educational difficulties?"

"I can't imagine. Not enough statues to defunct chefs?"

"You're close: not enough luncheon parties given by undergraduates in their rooms—of the sort Auden had at Oxford."

"Oh, yes," Kate said:

> *"Ah! those Twenties before I was twenty*
> *When the news never gave one the glooms,*
> *When the chef had minions in plenty,*
> *And we could have lunch in our rooms.*

Never having had lunch in my room, I wouldn't know. But Auden and I do have one oddity in common: we both grew so accustomed, as children, to being the youngest person present that even today we are likely to feel the youngest person in the room even if, as frequently happens, we are the oldest."

"Speaking of news giving one the glooms, as I suppose we must sooner or later," Clemance said, "I gather that you are supporting this University College, which I'm afraid I have always thought of as an extension school. I'm told that, unlike my colleagues Professors Cudlipp and O'Toole, you actually think the University College has greater value than the undergraduate college which I attended and where I teach. Cudlipp and O'Toole are both convinced that an undergraduate college for, as they put it, dropouts will undermine the value of any other undergraduate degree given in this University. I take it you don't agree with that?"

"No," Kate said, "I don't. Why should you have thought I would?"

Clemance laughed. "A good question," he said. "Why indeed? Kate Fansler, if I were to ask you, very rapidly, what you remember first of all, right off, about your childhood, what would you answer? You know, answer as in those association games we always used to hear so much about."

"Rose petals," Kate said.

Clemance looked surprised.

"Yes, odd as it may seem, and not for the world would I admit it to my revolutionary students, but I remember rose petals in the bottom of finger bowls, even at Nantucket where we spent the summers. When I was a child growing up, there was a depression and then a war; yet it might have been the Edwardian era, when, as everyone knows, the sun always shone. We had a cook in the house in New York and in Nantucket, a laundress who sat for hours at a mangle, maids running up and down the stairs, and finger bowls at dinner with rose petals in the bottom. My brothers were away at school, and then at war; I had a governess. Does all that matter?"

"It's very Proustian."

"So I've begun to think. Although the Duchess of Guermantes would always have been strange to me, I could have known Aunt Leonie and the two country walks, and the hawthorn blossoms. Does this have some connection with University College that I don't understand?"

Clemance sat forward in his chair and pursed his lips in thought, evolving one of his deliberate sentences which would emerge only slowly. "I went to a public high school for bright boys," he said, "and when I came to the College it was only because I got a partial scholarship and could live at home, and because my parents had carefully saved money over the years so that I might come here rather than to City College. I know that the City College classes of my time and later produced some of the most brilliant men in our country, but there was something here I cherished which I can only call graciousness, and a kind of excellence which was not alone determined by ambition. I find I am offended by the manners, by the lack of culture in the deepest sense of the word, prevalent today. I think in order to give everyone an opportunity, we are sacrificing our gifted people." Clemance made an impatient gesture with his hand. "I'm rambling," he said. "I can't think why I should have imagined you would know what I'm talking about."

"The instinct was quite correct," Kate said. "I can't bear bad manners and being called by my first name by strangers, yet I also realize that superficial good manners may cover the most appalling nastiness and hostility. My brothers have excellent manners, but they are basically the rudest men I have ever met. You see, I'm rambling too. My rudest graduate student went through Princeton on a complete scholarship, and as far as I can see he communicates either in dialectics or exponibles, part of a 'mechanized generation to whom haphazard oracular grunts are profound wisdom.' Do you suppose the University College students to be ruder than those in your own college? That isn't my impression."

"Perhaps I don't mean to talk about manners. Perhaps I mean to talk about excellence."

"There I am with you. But Professor Clemance, academic excellence is not that easily measurable. More and more students are getting perfect scores on college entrance tests—my graduate student with the oracular grunts scored very high indeed—but excellence is otherwise measurable, provided one maintains a minimum admissions score. The graduates of University College go on to graduate school in large numbers, astonishingly large numbers if one remembers the average age of the students. I know that some of those older students, especially the older women students, bore the boys in your college if they turn up in the same classes but, to be frank, the boys in your college bore me. I have never found youthful male arrogance, even when combined with great talent, especially appealing, while you, of course, have. In that, I suspect, we don't agree at all."

"You are accusing me simply of prejudice."

"Oh, yes, quite simply. And as to manners, your college boys have fewer of those. They were the original, uri-nating-on-the-President's-rug revolutionaries who called policemen pigs and the administration a double-barreled epithet I will not embarrass either of us by repeating. What I find difficult to understand is what it is you fear so about the University College—all of you, I mean. Those who are not satisfied to hurl from prep school through college and graduate school into the family law firm or whatever seem to me intelligent; it is surely the better part of wisdom to take time to think, and a country like ours should have a college for those who have gained wisdom and decided on a later, different college, or on a chance for a second life."

"Miss Fansler, could your University College have produced Auden?"

"No. And neither could your college, Professor Clemance." (Kate, as an inheritance from days when children were "brought up," found she could not bring herself to call Clemance "Frederick," a difficulty which Reed, who had never had a governess, thought preposterous.) "Oxford didn't produce Auden, even if it did allow him luncheon parties; neither did his doctor father, from whose books Auden used to learn the facts of life he diagrammed on the school-room blackboards, nor his mother, whom he loved and resembled. What produces an Auden? Having a friend like Isherwood when you are young?"

"Wouldn't you like it if Auden were to dedicate one of his poems to you?"

"I've given up daydreaming. No, I should always be so hideously frightened, with Auden, of being a bore or a hideola. Imagine afterward; one would have to drown oneself to avoid the memories."

"He's not as forbidding as all that; he's a superb teacher, you know."

"All I know about his teaching is another peculiarity we have in common: we are the only two teachers of literature who have ever admitted in class that we have never read *Don Quixote* through to the end."

"It is a good thing I didn't know that before I voted for your tenure."

"Professor Clemance, I have often wished for the opportunity to tell you that you taught me more—about literature, something I can only call morality, and about the honor of the profession of letters—than anyone else in the University. But you seemed to wish only for young male followers, and I did not wish to burden you with an older female disciple. Surely you must know, however, that no teacher knows where his influence reaches."

"I remember that you did a paper on *Portrait of a Lady*. I have never especially cared for women students. I think perhaps I was wrong in that. Perhaps there are Isabel Archers at University College."

Kate looked at him for a time. "Perhaps there are," she said. "I hope there isn't anything terribly wrong—with you, I mean?"

"But there is," he said. "My heart is broken. I have a pain in it." Kate remembered how he was always able to say dramatic things simply, as though emotion did not frighten him. "This student revolution hasn't broken your heart, hasn't affected your love for the University?"

"No," Kate said. "Much as I loved the rose petals in the finger bowls, I know my brothers too well. I have never cared for playboys or reactionaries, and they were produced by the same process that produced the finger bowls. I love talent, but do not care for privilege which takes itself for granted. To put it another way, I do not care for a society which has a place for Oblonsky, but none for Anna and Vronsky."

"What about Levin?"

"Levin without his estate and serfs would have been Anna. We are all Anna now."

Clemance sat silent for a time. "There is a Departmental meeting on Monday," he finally said. "No doubt the whole matter," he waved his hand in a familiar gesture, "will come up."

"No doubt."

"Jeremiah Cudlipp and Robert O'Toole feel very strongly about it; very strongly."

"So I have heard," she said. "Professor Clemance, let me tell you some non-University news: I'm to be married."

"Are you indeed? I am glad. It is good 'to be reborn, reneighbored in the Country of Consideration.' "

"The Country of Consideration: what a lovely definition of marriage."

"Yes," Clemance said. "If one considers it in the middle years, the best definition I know."

When Kate had parted from Clemance outside the Faculty Club, she walked for a time around the campus; the autumn was her favorite season, she was to have dinner with Reed, she was happy. The campus looked peaceful, benign, perhaps falsely so, but "when was peace or its concomitant smile the worse for being undeserved?" Perhaps, she thought, Reed will be ready early.

She was surprised, though only mildly so, to find McQuire waiting for her at the bus stop.

"More propositions?" Kate asked.

"I am Frogmore's pander. I promised him I would try to bring you over to the Club for a conversation. We've heard the English Senior Faculty Committee meeting is Monday, and we'd like a word in your ear before then."

"I have only just been at the Club," Kate said; "inferior lunch, superior quotations. I never even expected to be here Saturday when I took up this line of work."

"Come back to the Club with me now. I faithfully promise this will be the last time I abduct you."

. . .

"By the way," Kate said, as they walked toward the Faculty Club, "what's your great interest in the University College? Surely there aren't enough beautiful young things to be worth all this bother."

"Well—the University College these days is an extraordinarily vital place, while the College, let's face it, is catering first to a lot of boys fed up with work in prep schools whose only ambition for their college years is to get confronted and laid, preferably on alternate days, and second to the college alumni who want Alma Mater to go on unchanged, supporting the same prejudices and enthusiasms they remember, or think they do, from their undergraduate days. As an economist, I'm interested in the economically viable, and in the long run I think that's an adult undergraduate school. Certainly in New York City. I mean, it may be lovely to go and gambol by the Charles, but the river in this city is not a river but an estuary of the ocean, and it follows the tides of the ocean. I think we should stop trying to be Harvard or Yale and find our own pattern. I ought to add that St. Jude is my favorite saint: he of the lost causes—or has the Church demoted him along with the others?"

"All causes are lost causes, as e.e. cummings used to say; otherwise, they're effects."

Frogmore greeted Kate with all the exuberance of a hostess who had not really expected the guest of honor to appear. "Nevermind how goody-good he comes on," McQuire had said. "It's no doubt due to an oppressive upbringing. I have actually heard him use four-letter words, when driven. I don't know why University College should be a personal matter to him, but I think he would do almost anything for the sheer joy of seeing Cudlipp's face when the Board of Governors announce that they have voted to let University College continue." Today Frogmore ("Call me Vivian," he said to Kate, who was astonished; it seemed to her that any man named Vivian would stick to last names as a mere matter of survival) did not come on goody-good very long. "You'll never guess what that son-of-a—I beg your pardon, Kate—has done," he said. "Managed to get one of his pals in as Dean of the College."

"From the English Department? Do I know him? Or is his name unmentionable?"

"His name's O'Toole," Frogmore said. "Robert J. O'Toole. Ring a bell?"

"I don't believe it," Kate said. "Why should Robert O'Toole take a job like that? He's already a full professor and a leader of what I believe is known as the New York intellectual community, with influence even in certain parts of Connecticut and New Jersey. Why should he take . . . ?"

"Cudlipp has managed it. Of course, O'Toole's acceptable to the faculty because he's a name, and has a lot of university and extra-university weight to throw around. The only members of the College faculty who might have objected are those who can't stand O'Toole's guts, or those who don't think he's quite as good as he thinks he is . . ."

"Which is impossible on the face of it, from all I hear," McQuire interjected.

"And these, of course, were quietly persuaded by Cudlipp that it takes a . . ."

"Conceited, arrogant, insensitive bastard to win this fight," McQuire happily concluded. "Forgive me finishing all your sentences, Frogmore, but they all have such provocative beginnings."

"Which explains, I guess," Kate said, "why you want someone in the English Department on your side at the meeting Monday. Let's think about the English Department a moment, may we, if you can bear it?"

"That, Kate, is what I hoped you would say," Frogmore said, leaning toward her. "McQuire here can probably handle the Economics Department, but they will only give a certain amount of trouble—economists today, except for Bill, aren't really interested in undergraduate education —but if we can't do a little something in your department, Kate, we might as well turn in our badges. What will you drink?"

"Beer," Kate said. "It will remind me of how pleasant the park was this morning. O.K. We have Cartier committed to the University College, and also, if I may put order before modesty, you have me. Opposed to the University College you have Cudlipp, Clemance, O'Toole. But O'Toole as Dean will be off the College faculty. It's scarcely worth the price to us since he will be leading the fight in the main arena, but the odds on our side are small enough so that every advantage counts. From the rest of the Department we have the chairman, Michaels, who is, I would say, so fed up with Cudlipp and Clemance going over his head to the Acting President that he would probably welcome, in a properly decorous way, any plan which gave him some weight against those two. Everglade, the Secretary of the Department, is absolutely the sweetest guy in the world, but I don't really know what corner he'll be in. Probably ours. We have then Professor Peter Packer Pollinger, who is perfectly capable of voting on either side when it comes right down to it, depending on what he imagines Fiona Macleod would have done under similar circumstances, but as a matter of fact he dislikes Clemance so much for once having said that Fiona Macleod was a silly poetess whose rhymes were not improved by the fact that she was really a man that Professor Pollinger may vote with us if he remembers what it was Clemance said on the day he happens to vote."

"Kate, dear," McQuire interrupted, "I do hope you know what you're talking about. Frogmore and I aren't going to ask you to explain why a lady poet should be a man, but you might just assure us that you aren't, shall we say, rambling?"

"I assure you. The one who rambles is Peter Packer Pollinger. All right, then we have Chaucer, Medieval English, Comparative Medieval, Renaissance, Seventeenth Century, Eighteenth Century, Shakespeare. I don't know where any of them stands (I mention the fields rather than the names for the moment to give you the scope of the problem) but the older the field, the more conservative the views, as a general rule. The only trouble with that is that I'm not certain what they'll consider the conservative position in this case. Of the two people in the contemporary field, one is Plimsole, who is a College man and lost, I fear, to us, but he is so unbelievably long-winded that I can't believe even the College will consider him altogether an asset, though he's not a bad fellow if he could learn to stop talking when he gets to the end of what he wants to say. The other contemporary person is Emilia Airhart."

"You must be putting us on. I never heard of her, I mean not as a member of the English Department. You aren't suggesting she made it out of the Oriental waters only to pop up here in a new life."

"I hadn't realized, really, what an odd lot we were. Emilia's little known because she never turns up anywhere except to see students, whom she likes, and to write plays, which keep getting put on off-Broadway, but they are so very with it that no one in the whole Department realized for years that Emilia was writing them. She never has anything to do with anything in the Department, never goes to parties or gives them; she *might* come down on our side on this issue—it's not unlikely."

"What does she look like?" Frogmore said. "I thought I knew all the tenured English faculty."

"What she looks like is the whole point, as you'd realize the moment you clapped eyes on her. She's a large woman with flat shoes, wide skirts, and glasses, who gives you the

impression that she could actually be a *jolie laide* if someone with the combined talents of Sophie Gimbel and Yves
St. Laurent would only take her in hand. She's got five
children and a husband, and that's almost all I know about
her, although I know her better than most people, since
we're the only two women with tenure in the Department
and we inevitably find ourselves together in the ladies'
room from time to time. Her specialty's drama, and the
only other thing I know about her is that when I once
asked her what she thought of Clemance, she said that
apart from the fact that he was pompous, a company man
and a male chauvinist, she had nothing against him, which
I suppose, is another good sign for us. All the rest of the
Department don't have votes on the Senior Faculty Committee, being non-tenure, and need not concern us, though
of course they wield more influence than is often realized.
I hope I have made it quite clear that this is going to be
an uphill fight."

"You don't know how uphill," McQuire said. "It's on the
question of promotions that I've had my troubles with the
Economics Department. The point is, we want you to see
that a couple of assistant professors who've been teaching
at the University College get promoted."

"You don't want much, do you?" Kate asked.

"The thing about Frogmore," McQuire said, "is that
easy fights bore him."

"Listen, Kate," Frogmore said, "I don't want to be
Dean of University College if it gets a new image, a new
lease on life, and a new destiny. I want to be president of
a girls' college somewhere very rural and genteel. But I
want to see University College the model of elite adult
education for the whole United States, and I want it so
badly that I'm going to get it."

"What odd reasoning," Kate said.

"No, it's not," Frogmore said. "When you find a man

who wants something very badly, and doesn't want it for himself, watch out."

Kate stared at Frogmore awhile. "Do you know, Vivian," she said, "like the man, meaning McQuire here, said, you got guts."

"What happens at that Senior Faculty Committee meeting on Monday is going to show us a lot," Frogmore said.

"I can hardly wait," Kate laughed.

Then she hurried home to Reed.

CHAPTER
FIVE

There will be no peace.
Fight back, then, with such courage as you have
And every unchivalrous dodge you know of,
  Clear in your conscience on this:
Their cause, if they had one, is nothing to them now;
  They hate for hate's sake.

Monday, Kate reached Baldwin at two, in time for her office hour. The Senior Faculty Committee meeting was scheduled for four that afternoon, and Kate hoped, without too much conviction, to pick up a few tips before the meeting on the way the wind was blowing. So political a thought had not previously occurred to her and marked, no doubt, her initiation into the world of history. Clio, she thought, stand me now and ever in good stead.

"We have found no one for Swahili," a voice said. "How is Bulwer-Lytton doing? Look, the elevator is actually coming," Mark Everglade added. "There must be something wrong with it."

"I do think," Kate said as they got in, pressed '8' and watched the doors close, "that such consistent pessimism is surely the triumph of experience over hope, not to mention reason. Even this University's elevators must work occasionally. The law of averages . . ." Kate's voice faded away as, between the third and fourth floors, the elevator came to a reluctant, but by no means uncertain, stop.

"There is a law of averages," Everglade said. "There is also a law of falling bodies. We are about to prove Galileo's theory that two bodies of different weights will, if dropped from a sufficient height, reach the ground at the same time and in the same state of dejectedness. You ring the alarm bell; I will telephone."

Kate pressed the alarm bell in much the same spirit with which one accepts herbal tea from an ancient aunt: it probably won't help, but it can't hurt. Mark, meanwhile, addressed himself to a little cupboard which housed the University's most recent attempt to grapple with the problem of its elevators: a telephone. "What do you dial for emergencies?" Mark asked Kate.

"I don't know. It says in the front of the campus directory, but I'm afraid I never noticed."

"Who, alas, has? We shall have to dial the operator, and we all know where that leads."

"Do you think there is sufficient oxygen?"

"For what? Compared to the air I've been breathing in most meetings lately, there is probably here a smaller proportion of carbon monoxide and irritating tars than in most otherwheres."

"May I help you?" a voice said over the telephone.

"You certainly may," Mark happily replied. "We are stuck in an elevator and . . ."

"If you are on campus," the voice continued, "you may dial directly the number you want. Is this an outside call?"

"I can't even get outside this elevator," Mark said. "Help, help, help," he mildly added.

"I will connect you with maintenance," the voice said. "If you are on campus, will you dial one-two, one-four? Are you on campus?"

"Perhaps it's a recording," Kate said.

Mark pressed down the telephone button until he heard a dial tone, then dialed 1214. There was a busy signal.

"Try calling the English Office," Kate said.

"A brilliant suggestion which I am hideously certain will not work. Ah, well." Mark dialed the English Office.

"English," the secretary's voice brightly said, "will you hold on a minute?" There was a click as the secretary pushed the 'hold' button. Mark slammed the receiver down as violently as the small cupboard allowed. Kate put her purse and case down on the floor.

"I am reminded," she said, "of a story my father used to tell, repeatedly, in order to drive home a moral whose application has, until this moment, escaped me. He was a friend of the president of some railroad, the New York Central or something, and one day my father asked his secretary to find out when the next train left for Tuxedo, where he was planning to meet someone. The secretary returned to tell him that she could not get through to railroad information because the line was continually engaged. 'Nonsense,' my father called out. 'Get me the president of the whatever railroad.' The poor secretary couldn't get the president, but she did get his private secretary, at which point my father grabbed the telephone from her. 'I'm terribly sorry, Mr. Fansler,' the president's private secretary said, 'but Mr. Whosis is out of town. Is there any way I can help you?' 'There certainly is,' my father said; 'when is the next train to Tuxedo?' Well, she managed to find a timetable and tell him; and the moral of the story is: always go to the president."

"I trust," Mark said, "that since we are without a President, the Acting President will do."

"Perfectly," Kate said.

"And do you happen to know his extension?"

"Yes, I do. I was recently glancing through the new directory, as one does when it first comes out, and I noticed that his number is 1837. Shall we try it?"

"How did you happen to decide to remember his number and not the emergency number? Your father's advice?"

"Naturally not. I have never given a thought to my father's advice until this moment. Eighteen thirty-seven is the year of Queen Victoria's ascension."

"Of course. Silly of me." Mark picked up the receiver and dialed 1837.

"President Matthewson's office," a voice cheerfully said. "Good afternoon."

"Good afternoon," Mark said. "May I please speak to Mr. Matthewson? This is Mark Everglade of the English Department calling."

"I'm terribly sorry, Mr. Everglade, but President Matthewson is at a meeting. May I take a message?"

"You certainly may," Mark said. "Tell him that Professor Fansler and I, both of the English Department, are stuck in an elevator in Baldwin Hall and are rapidly running out of oxygen. I might add, in case it will in any way goad you more rapidly to action, that Professor Fansler and I are not of the same sex. Good afternoon to *you*." Mark hung up the phone. "I give her fifteen minutes," Mark said, "to check on us and the elevator. Shall we go over the catalogue, since the opportunity presents itself?"

"Mark, what do you think of Cudlipp?"

"He does his job, which is to represent the College. I do mine, which is to represent the Graduate School. Michaels, as chairman of the whole Department, complains about Cudlipp from time to time, but after all, everybody's got to do his thing, doesn't he?"

"I often ask myself," Kate said, "—does he? Do you know anything about University College?"

"Sure," Mark surprisingly said. "I've been letting its students into my classes lately; they're good."

"Funny, you never mentioned it," Kate said.

"To tell you the truth, I'm not certain it's kosher, so it seemed a case of least said soonest mended."

"Do you think Cudlipp would object if he knew?"

"No doubt. But he can't very well do anything about it, since the Graduate School doesn't give credit, and what credit the University College gives is its decision. He makes damn sure no University College students take any College courses, or vice versa, and that's exactly as far as he can go."

"Why is he so against the University College? I know all about the question of resources, but his passion has deeper roots than the University's operating deficit."

"Mainly, I guess, he thinks the University College degree threatens the value of *The* College degree. He wants undergraduate education at the University to be absolutely elite, and all those adults returning with their tired brains to school threaten him."

"Do I," Kate asked, "hear the calls of rescuers?"

"Professor Everglade," a voice called. "Switch the Emergency button to *off*, and push open the door."

Mark looked at Kate and shrugged. "Well," he said, "here goes. Are you prepared to dive down the shaft?" He switched the button and pushed at the inner door which, rather to his astonishment, opened. Below them, the door on the third floor had been pushed back. "Have you a lady in there?" the voice called. "Professor Fansler is with me," Mark said, winking at Kate, "if that answers your question. The point, I gather," he said to Kate, "is to drop down into their arms on the third floor but *not* into the elevator shaft. Chivalry demands that you go first, so that I may hand you down into their waiting arms. And we never even looked at the damn catalogue."

It was typical of Kate's post-revolutionary attitudes that being caught in an elevator, which might, at one time, have been an adventure, was now not even material for an anecdote. She rushed up the stairs from the third floor to her office on the eighth, apologized for her lateness, and plunged into interviews with four students from University College who hoped to register for her course in Victorian literature. She recognized John Peabody from the luncheon arranged by Bill McQuire. He introduced the others: Barbara Campbell, Greta Gabriel, and Randolph Selkirk. "No doubt," Mr. Peabody said, "you want to know something about us, how we come to be at University College, why we want to take your course, stuff like that. It's probably simplest if we just start in and tell you about ourselves." To Kate, who had been uncertain what inquiries she might decently make, given, particularly, her profound disinclination to ask personal questions, this blunt prelude was a distinct relief.

"We," Mr. Peabody began, "have all returned to college after what is known as a voluntary interruption in our education—though the word voluntary has to be pretty broadly defined. Anyway, we weren't bounced out of college, we bounced ourselves. And when, in the fullness of time, we decided to return to college, the last thing we wanted was dormitory life, rah-rah games, anybody being *in loco parentis* or the company of eighteen-year-olds. To us, therefore, University College seemed a kind of miracle. There aren't many adult schools in the whole country, not many even in New York—schools which give degrees, and aren't just places to take courses and wile away the time. University College has no athletic requirements, no organized social life, and some of us are a bit shaky at math at the time of our entrance examination. But we are all in college because we have decided to be; we are, as the saying goes, highly motivated; and most of us are even pretty bright. I might add, though Barbara can tell you more about this, that the women students are looking for a bachelor's degree, not for a bachelor."

Barbara Campbell was stunning, beautifully dressed, and appeared to be in her early twenties. "I'm fairly typical, I guess," she said with a smile which acknowledged that she certainly didn't look typical. "I went to an excellent prep school where I was mainly interested in what our antedeluvian headmistress used to call 'the lads,' and then to Bennington, where I spent three years— almost; I quit in the middle of my third year. I discovered at Bennington that I enjoyed thinking, and that if you work there are plenty of people who will encourage you. I worked like a demon for five days, when, since we were all girls, it wasn't necessary to wash your hands or feet or even face if you didn't feel like it, and every weekend I spent away from the campus with a man.

"Partly, I began to realize that I had been in an intel- lectual and emotional cocoon for years, and partly I just wanted to *bouleverse les parents*—at which I succeeded beyond my wildest expectations. They objected to the fact that I was living with a guy, they even objected to the guy, which at least made some sense, and they said if I didn't give him up they would stop paying for college or anything else. I didn't and they did. After a time I got tired of the guy, and of working in the glamour trades, and I began to want to study again. I saved enough money and here I am. My parents have since come round, but I don't take any money from them, though I have been known to accept an occasional lavish present. If I took their money they would assume, however tacitly, that I had accepted their values, and I haven't. I want to take your course because I've heard you're great, and tough, and it recently occurred to me how like a harem Bennington was. I don't mean just that all the faculty was sleeping with the stu- dents, I mean that all the faculty was male, and that the whole spirit behind the place was of girls sitting at the feet of men. I find the idea of a woman teacher invigorat- ing. End of my speech—I'm to introduce Greta."

Greta Gabriel was in her middle forties, Kate guessed. Her story resembled Polly Spence's, though she had not yet reached the grandmother phase and was not from the upper reaches of New York society. She was a suburban housewife who had decided that her life of being maid, chauffeur, and emotional wastebasket was insufficiently inspiring. Everything about her new academic life was difficult, from the commuting to the pressures of her life's multitudinous demands, but she felt alive for the first time in years, and indicated her gratitude for the uniqueness of University College, which allowed her really to work, not to dabble, and agreed to reward her work with a degree.

Randolph Selkirk was more unexpected. "I was at Yale," he said, "getting A's in everything and working all day six days a week to do it. I had a girl and one day she broke off with me, saying I wasn't human enough for her. It took me several weeks to calm down and discover it was quite true—I wasn't human enough for anyone. I stopped working so hard, and finally took a leave from Yale and went to work teaching in a slum school; then I married the girl, who had begun to find me more human. We had a baby, which seemed to us a proper affirmation of life, and after a time I wanted to return to school, and this was the only place that wasn't an undergraduate society for boys or a series of money-making courses for bored adults. My wife is working to help me finish, and I can't begin to understand why they should want to get rid of this place—University College, I mean. Still, I've observed that the boys from the College are radical enough when it comes to occupying buildings, but not when it comes to supporting an institution which might challenge the status of their own degrees. I've noticed nobody minds being revolutionary when he doesn't think he has anything to lose. Forgive the cynicism. If you want to know why I'd like to take this course, it's because I'm particularly interested in the ideas of the Victorian period."

Kate leaned back in her chair and regarded the four of

them. It seemed to her, oddly, that life had walked into her academic world, impressing her as not even the police or occupying students had done. She understood why McQuire found impressive the fact that University College students had been the only ones to feel loyalty to their school. Of course, she had sensed it from the beginning—which was why she had let McQuire drag her to that lunch and entice her into conversations with Frogmore. " 'Your presence exactly,' " Kate thought, looking at them, " 'so once, so valuable, so very now.' "

"You are welcome to the course," she simply said.

What with further student conferences, a delegation from the student-faculty committee on curriculum, a good many frantic telephone calls, and similar distractions, Kate was not able even to ascertain if there was a wind, let alone the direction in which it was blowing. At four o'clock, the hour of the Senior Faculty Committee meeting, she left her office and stopped off in the faculty ladies' room where she found Emilia Airhart looking at herself dubiously in a mirror. She turned, apparently with relief, to contemplate Kate. "How lucky you are!" she surprisingly said.

"I?" Kate asked. "I'm feeling lucky at the moment, for personal reasons. Does it show?"

Emilia Airhart laughed. "Probably," she said, "but I don't know you well enough to tell. Congratulations, whatever it is. The luck to which I referred had to do with your willowyness—I have always longed to be willowy; if only one could design oneself, instead of turning out to be some dreadful preordained shape. I would, like you, be tall and slim, with my hair gathered at the nape of my neck, attractive without being charming. You mustn't be insulted by the last item, which is, from me, a compliment. I dislike charm, having accepted Camus' definition of it: the ability to get the answer *yes* without having asked a question. I prefer people who have to form questions. Still, it is agonizing to have the soul of Greta Garbo in the body of Queen Victoria. Ergo, lucky you."

Kate laughed. "You don't look a bit like Queen Victoria," she said.

"Of course I do, if you could picture Queen Victoria in panty hose with flat shoes and her skirts above her knees. I take it you are going to the Senior Faculty Committee meeting?"

"Yes," Kate said. "And for once in my life I don't wish I could think of an excuse not to. I go with a purpose: I've decided to do what I can for the University College. Do you know anything about it?"

"Haven't a clue; ought I to have?"

"Probably," Kate said. "But there isn't time to go into it now. The College is trying to kill it off, which is rather too bad, I think."

"Nasty old Cudlipp, I suppose. Terrible man. If only he were more like Pnin."

"Who?"

"You know, Pnin, the man in Nabokov's novel. Cudlipp looks just like him, but, alas, couldn't be more different. I hardly like to say that if Cudlipp and Clemance are for something, I'm against it—it sounds so unscholarly and prejudiced, which it is—but at least I'm leaning in your direction, if that's any comfort."

"It's some," Kate said. "By the way, as to my being lucky, I'm getting married. I haven't told anyone in the Department yet, but I'll have to soon. Perhaps it's being unmarried that's kept me thin."

"Congratulations, or whatever the proper phrase is, though in a way I'm sorry." Kate raised an interrogative eyebrow. "Don't misunderstand me, but you're the only woman I've ever known who seemed unmarried as a wonderful choice, the combined influence of Artemis, Aphrodite, and Athene all in one. Please don't be offended."

"On the contrary," Kate said. "I'm honored." Emilia gave a pleased grin and preceded Kate out the door. But Kate stopped a moment in the hall. "You know," she said, "Forster says in one of his novels that the abandonment of personality can be a prelude to love; for most women I think it certainly is. You've made me see that, for me, it hasn't been."

"Do you like Forster?" Emilia Airhart asked. "I see you do; he's too effete for me. But he did say once that life is a performance on a violin which one has to learn to play as he goes along. A remarkable description of our times."

"Gentle, perhaps," Kate said, "not effete."

The Senior Faculty Committee of the English Department, which comprised all tenured members of the Department, used, in pre-revolutionary days, to meet several times a semester for the purpose of discussing promotions and additions to the faculty. While these meetings were grim enough, in all conscience, a certain degree of cordiality prevailed, so that, as Kate used to say, though it might be clear that one professor thought another a tiresome, pontificating, and deluded bore, he did not openly indicate this opinion. Since last spring, however, fatigue and the plethora of meetings which the process of restructuring inevitably entailed had taken their hostages, which were, as always, good will, courtesy, and graciousness. The professors were exhausted, and exhausted people are easily made first angry and then rude.

To make matters worse, exhaustion bred not only bad temper but long-windedness. The inability of certain men, once they had got to their feet, to finish a statement and sit down, amounted, in Kate's view, to a disease as incurable as satyriasis and far more socially dangerous. She knew, as she seated herself in the room, that scarcely would Michaels, the chairman, have rustled his papers and made the few desperate grunts, punctuated by giggles, which constituted his reaction to exhaustion, than Plimsole would be on his feet and away. In fact, he was.

Plimsole was concerned, as he had been for months, as to whether teaching assistants should be considered primarily as students, which they were, or as teachers, which they were also. The question was certainly of importance and was one, moreover, on which the radical faculty felt a consuming passion the conservative faculty was not prepared to match. This, perhaps more than anything else, annoyed Professor Plimsole. Kate could well infer from the looks on the faces of those about her that had the senior faculty had an opportunity to hear Mr. Plimsole before his promotion, that event might well have never taken place. It was, Kate thought, a mark of the need for this revolution that the faculty of departments like this never met, and the senior members never really heard the junior members at all. But, since last spring, all the meetings except those of the Senior Faculty Committees had been open to junior faculty and the long-winded Mr. Plimsoles might in the future be more successfully nipped in the bud.

"I really do feel," Mr. Plimsole began, "that this body must come to a decision about the professional autonomy of teaching assistants. It is not that I anticipate another series of events like those which rocked this institution last spring; indeed, I would hate my colleagues to think I spoke in anticipation or even expectation of any such event, but I also do feel that we cannot allow our teaching assistants to remain in doubt as to their actual professional standing, and they are professionals, we must face that, for certainly the teaching assistants come into direct contact with students, both in actual teaching duties and in the correction of papers, and it is surely insufferable and insulting that they should be loaded with the responsibilities of teaching and then be treated as students if they are found, for example, occupying a building, though as I

76

have indicated I do not bring this subject up because I think buildings are likely to be occupied in the near future. But once we have co-opted them into our profession they must be treated professionally and not summarily dismissed as teachers because as students they have acted against what they consider inequitable policies on the part of the administration, whether or not those of us here consider the policies of the recent administration to have been inequitable or not . . ."

"His hat!" Emilia Airhart, who had risen, shouted. "His hat!" For a moment there was stunned silence as everyone tried to absorb the evident fact that Professor Airhart had flipped; Mr. Plimsole was certainly not wearing a hat, discourtesy having failed, as yet, to extend that far. Professor Airhart, having delivered her interruption, sat down again. Mr. Plimsole, as though he were an old mechanical Victrola, could be seen, metaphorically speaking, to be winding himself up again. But Professor Cartier, whose succinctness no revolution could undermine, bounced up just in time.

"Mrs. Airhart, whose field is contemporary drama, refers to a speech by a character called Lucky in *Waiting for Godot*: those of you interested in the reference may have time to look it up this evening if this meeting is allowed to get on with its agenda. I congratulate Mrs. Airhart on the appositeness of her remarks, and remind Mr. Plimsole that the question of teaching assistants occupying buildings is properly the business of the Committee on Graduate Studies. I would like to put before *this* committee the promotion of Professors Levy and Genero, presently teaching in the University College." He sat down as abruptly as he had stood up. Kate grinned. She remembered, as no doubt did all her colleagues, Lucky's speech, which, while it made less syntactical sense than Mr. Plimsole's, achieved at least the adumbration of significance.

Cartier's remark, as was inevitable, brought Jeremiah Cudlipp to his feet. "If Mr. Plimsole's contentions are misplaced before this committee, and I agree that they are [glare at Mr. Plimsole which Kate wanted to regret for his sake, but could not], so are those of Mr. Cartier. Assistant professors teaching in the University College cannot be considered for tenure by this committee until it is established that the University College is, in fact, a continuing part of the University. I suggest that it is not a continuing part, and ought not so to be considered by this committee." He sat down. Kate heaved a sigh. The fat was in the fire or, as McQuire would have said, the four-letter-word-bathroom had hit the fan. Michaels, the chairman, giggled, rustled his papers, and drew in his breath to speak. In vain. Clemance had risen to his feet.

"I support Professor Cudlipp," he said, as though that might be news to anyone, "but," and every head in the room came expectantly up, "I think perhaps we ought honestly to confront the problem before us. I have a sense of polarization having divided this committee, and that sense is profoundly disturbing to me. I think we ought to listen to what Professor Cartier has to say, and indeed to what any of us may have to say on this question, even if we cannot today vote to recommend the promotion of people in a school which may not for long exist."

At this precise moment—it was probably not planned that way, but Kate wouldn't put it past them—the door opened and Robert O'Toole entered. The myrmidons were gathering. Kate looked at Clemance. Why, she thought, is your conscience bothering you? Bless you. Robert O'Toole's thoughts, however, were clearly far from wishing to convey a blessing.

"I'm afraid I can't agree with Frederick," O'Toole said, calling Clemance by his first name. "It seems to me inevitable that his great-heartedness should lead him to such a sense of openness, and equally inevitable that we, his more narrow-minded friends, should recall him to the fundamental accuracy of things."

Professor Cartier again rose to his feet. "Mr. O'Toole's ability to answer questions he hasn't heard is certainly worthy of admiration. I should like to repeat my recommendation that we consider for possible promotion Professor Levy. He has done excellent work in the Victorian field, and if I understand correctly departmental needs at the moment, we could use a man in the Victorian period."

"I thought Professor Levy's book on Wilkie Collins excellent," Michaels said. "Have any of the rest of you read it?"

"I have," O'Toole said, extending his arms from his French cuffs and examining his fingernails. "It's a good enough book in its way, modest, unexceptional, competent, but small in its ambition. One can't condemn it nor, I think, is one inclined to praise it extravagantly." At this point someone tapped Kate's shoulder and handed her a note; it said, "Whatever that pompous s.o.b. is for, I'm against. EA." Kate grinned her appreciation of the sentiments expressed, and stuffed the paper into her purse. Several senior professors now began to argue about Mr. Levy's book and Kate, sensing some moments' respite, rested her eyes on Clemance. Was O'Toole, in a sense, a comment on Frederick Clemance, an inevitable commentary which now, like the notes to "The Waste Land," had to be considered along with the original document? O'Toole had been one of Clemance's most brilliant, most loved students, and had returned the affection wholeheartedly, not least by adopting every mannerism of Clemance's for his own. But he could never learn to temper his arrogance as Clemance had learned. Or would he learn in time? When Kate had first known Clemance, after all, when she had first sat in his seminar, Clemance had been almost as near to fifty as O'Toole was now to forty. Could ten years make that much difference? Kate doubted it.

The news of O'Toole's deanship was apparently not yet general. But that O'Toole had himself decided that the success of his tenure depended upon the demise of the University College was beyond question. At this point Professor Peter Packer Pollinger could be heard sputtering through his mustache; slowly the group's attention focused on him. "Why's he against it?" Professor Pollinger was asking the world in general.

"Are you addressing me, sir?" Clemance mildly asked.

" 'What is it that is moving so softly to and fro?' I asked," Professor Pollinger said.

Clemance regarded Professor Pollinger as though, were sufficient attention paid, some meaning might be discerned; the hope, however, proved illusory. "Is that a quotation," he patiently asked, "perhaps from some misty Maeterlinck-like drama?" This question, which was not intended to be, and was not delivered as though it was, insulting, aroused Professor Peter Packer Pollinger to the highest reaches of indignation.

"Mist be damned," he said. "It is a question of symbolism, whoever you are. Same as the English toward the Irish; pure snobbism. That adult college is a symbol to you, and you and you," he nodded, causing his mustache to quiver as he indicated Clemance, Cudlipp, and O'Toole. "I know the reason. Cudlipp went to University College himself when it was still just a group of extension courses, after they threw him out of the College and before they took him back. I thought Levy's book large and exceptional, and I am inclined to praise it extravagantly. You," he said to O'Toole, "are lost in an obscure wood." He puffed again through his mustache, leaving his on the whole pleased audience to infer that the obscure wood occurred in one of Miss Macleod's misty dramas.

"Surely," Clemance continued, "we are wandering rather from the point. At least," he added, anticipating another outburst, "from my point. Whatever our views may be on the University College, they are not the most germane points to be made at the present time. The Administrative Council has, I believe, undertaken to study the needs of the University as a whole. Doubtless we will all be asked to present our points of view, if any. Meanwhile, it seems to me perhaps irregular to consider promoting to tenure assistant professors whose service is entirely in a school whose future in the University is problematical."

Are you just trying to smooth it all over? Kate thought. She wondered if Peter Packer Pollinger's allegations against Cudlipp could possibly be true. Interesting. Professor Goddard, who taught medieval literature and whose specialty was *Piers Plowman*, rose to his feet.

"I don't follow Professor Clemance's reasoning at all. In the first place, it is our business to promote people on the basis of their ability and possible service to the Department, not on the future of any school in the University. In the second place, I am on the Council to which Professor Clemance refers, and I don't think I'm betraying any confidences by saying that the Council is also studying whether or not The College has a place today in an urban university like this, whose reputation has been made largely through its graduate offerings. I don't mind saying that my own inclination is to consider that a college for adults is more to the point in New York than a college for overgrown schoolboys from whose ranks, I need not remind all of you, came most of the instigators of last spring's disturbances."

Into the awed silence which followed this remark Kate spoke. "I wondered," she said, "how many of us here do, in fact, have students from University College in our classes. The College, as we know, has always avoided cross-listing courses with the Graduate School, but I have only recently learned that University College does, in fact, encourage students to enter many of our courses. How many here do have University College students in their classes?"

"I might add," Michaels said, "that such a show of hands will be unofficial, and its results not recorded in our minutes. Is it all right with you, Professor Fansler, if your question remains unrecorded too?"

"Certainly," Kate said. "I asked it for my own information, and so that I might follow it with another question, also off the record if you like, at least for the present: How good are those students?"

Tentatively at first, and then with more assurance as the number of hands in the air increased, the professors indicated the presence of University College students in their classes. Professor Peter Packer Pollinger was of course one of the first to raise a triumphant hand, whether because he knew it would annoy Clemance or because he had found a Macleod admirer was not, nor ever likely to be, clear. "And have you found them to be good students, or poor students, or merely satisfactory?"

"I object," Cudlipp shouted, running a hand over his bald head. He had a habit of throwing back his bald head as though he had, in fact, long hair which dangled in his eyes. "The question is irrelevant."

"Nonsense," Professor Goddard shouted, "*Piers Plowman* may, as my students persistently tell me, lack relevancy, but if you are damning a part of this University to extinction, I fail to see how it can be irrelevant to discuss the quality of its students. Perhaps Professor Cudlipp can enlighten me."

"Before Professor Cudlipp enlightens us," Michaels, the chairman, said, "may I be allowed a few words? I don't know if you are aware that I am running this Department, which is twice as big as the Business School, and almost twice as large as the Law School, with no administrative staff whatever—the Law School, I may remind you, has five deans, the Business School six—and I am teaching two courses in Victorian poets at the same time. Mr. Levy, whom, because he is in my field, I know better than I know Mr. Genero, would be able to help me considerably not only with my dissertation load, but with certain administrative tasks in the department. Though none of you can be expected to know it, Mr. Levy is a first-rate administrator. If we are to promote people·on the basis of their usefulness to the English Department, I would like to point out that, whatever the abilities of the students in the University College, Mr. Levy is to be highly recommended."

"I would like to second that," Mark Everglade said. "Mr. Genero, as it happens, is in my field, which is Comparative Renaissance, he is fluent in Italian and speaks and reads five other languages as well, and if I am to continue as Secretary I would like to suggest that his usefulness to me can scarcely be overestimated. Let me add, while I have the floor, that the students from University College who have been in my classes have been first-rate and have been, compared to the boys from the College, possessed of a higher degree of motivation and a considerably lower degree of arrogance."

Cudlipp leaped to his feet. "I move that this meeting be adjourned," he shouted.

"I second the motion," O'Toole said.

"Now wait a minute," Cartier shouted.

"Motions for adjournment are not debatable," Cudlipp announced. Indeed, the faculty had learned Robert's Rules of Order in recent months.

"We shall have to take a vote," Michaels said. "All in favor of adjournment signify by saying 'Aye.'" There was a loud chorus of 'Ayes.' "Opposed."

"No," several voices trumpeted.

"The 'Ayes' have it," Michaels said. "This meeting is adjourned." He gathered up his papers and marched from the room lest any inclination to continue the discussion manifest itself.

"Interesting," Kate said to Mark Everglade, "and thanks for your support."

"It was heartfelt," Mark said, "and not at all disinterested. I'm conniving for Genero's assistance in a desperate way."

"What astonished me," Kate said, "is how many we've obviously got on our side—the side, I mean, of University College. The support is much greater than I dared think. Of course, alas and alack, Cudlipp must be aware of this as fully as I. What do you think he'll do next?"

"What you taught me to do in the elevator," Everglade said, "remembering, in your Proustian way, the stories your father told." Kate stared at him. "He'll go straight to the President," Everglade explained, "together with Clemance, the University's most renowned adornment, and O'Toole, Dean of the College—yes, I was passed a note during the meeting. Speaking to the President directly works for getting out of elevators, discovering train schedules, and killing schools and promotions."

"Does Cudlipp really have that much power?"

"He does. What is more, all Michaels and I have been able to threaten him with is our resignations from the administrative posts in the Department we so reluctantly occupy; and since Cudlipp would be only too delighted to take on those duties himself, with all that means for his enemies, our threats can scarcely be dignified by the term idle."

"Golly," Kate said.

"So," Everglade asked, "what else is new?"

"As it happens," Kate said, "I'm getting married."

Enjoying the impact of this as a curtain line, Kate, who

was still eschewing elevators, ran down the stairs and out of Baldwin, again to meet Polly Spence.

"I was on my way to see you," Polly Spence said, "absolutely on my way. Have you *heard* the news from the Linguistics Department?"

"They've disproved Verner's Law," Kate ventured; "they've discovered long E never shifted after all."

"It's almost that amazing. They're firing the only specialist they have in the English language because they might have to give him tenure and he's primarily associated with University College."

"The words are familiar," Kate said, "and I even think I recognize the tune."

"Which will mean," Polly went on, "actually *mean* that the Linguistics Department will have a specialist in Chinese and *not* in English—can you believe it?"

"Oddly enough, I can," Kate said. "Who objects to the promotion from University College, have you heard?"

"Well, of course, I'm just a lowly teaching assistant, and none of my news can be called from the horse's mouth, or even from his immediate neighborhood, but the *general* word is that The College objects, and especially the new dean who looms on the horizon, though he is as yet nameless."

"I believe," Kate said, "I could put a name to him. Polly, you've actually come up with something lunch at the Cosmo wouldn't cure. Give my love to Winthrop and I'll give yours to Reed."

"Who's Reed?" Polly Spence called.

"My husband, more or less," Kate called back, leaving Polly open-mouthed and speechless on the steps of Baldwin Hall.

PART TWO

Death and After

CHAPTER SIX

Looking up at the stars, I know quite well
That, for all they care, I can go to hell,
But on earth indifference is the least
We have to dread from man or beast.

The news that Kate was acquiring a husband became, as the fall semester got under way, the excuse for a bacchanal. Which is to say that the three secretaries in the English Department, certain that marriage is more important than revolution, planned a department party to celebrate. Kate and Reed were to be the honored guests, and everyone who was invited would contribute the necessary funds and come. One may insult one's colleagues, the administration, or the Board of Governors, but one does not offend secretaries.

"You," Kate said to Reed, "are my greatest accomplishment. I have achieved the apotheosis of womanhood. To have earned a Ph.D., taught reasonably well, written books, traveled, been a friend and lover—these are mere evasions of my appointed role in life: to lead a man to the altar. You are my sacrifice to the goddess of middle-class morality, as Iphigenia was Agamemnon's sacrifice to Artemis. Shall you mind the party frightfully?"

"I shall be giddily amused. Nor had I known the victim enjoyed the sacrifice. I can never remember having been so outrageously happy."

"Which merely shows how even the sanest man can be

the sport of the gods. There are times, Reed, when I wonder if you know what you're taking on. But I suppose if one ever knew that, one would never do anything. May I urge you to back out, if you so choose, before the party? After it, you are more committed than if the banns had been read in St. Paul's Cathedral. Secretaries may not be trifled with."

"What I don't understand," Reed said, as they set out for the party, which was being held in the English Department Offices (thus making it semi-official and obviating the necessity of asking wives), "is what Clemance wanted from you at your lunch *à deux*."

"I expect he wanted reassurance," Kate said.

"Clearly; but of what?"

"That he need not change his ways; that those who felt impelled to kill the University College need not be stopped by him."

"But why should he have expected you to provide the reassurance?"

"That is the question, I know. I think it must have occurred to him that, suffering like him from heartache, I might be induced to back him up in his old-fashioned opinions, particularly since, as he suspected, I had an old-fashioned background whose beauty I was not prepared to deny. You see, his moral nature or his imagination or both caught him up. Of course, Emilia Airhart thinks that he is a male chauvinist and a company man, and if she's right, the University College may well be doomed, but I take his choosing to have lunch with me as a sign that she may be wrong."

"My instincts tell me not to ask, but I will ignore them; who is Emilia Airhart?"

"You'll meet her tonight—the only other lady member of the department, of tenure rank that is, and therefore on the secretaries' most exclusive list. I think you'll like her, if you don't object to large, downright women on principle. She likes me because she thinks me willowy."

"You are," Reed said. "The willowiest of the willowy."

It was with some trepidation that Kate agreed to take the elevator to the eighth floor. After her dramatic presentations about the wild eccentricities of University elevators, Reed was mildly disappointed to arrive at the English Department with no undue incident whatever. He was immediately taken in tow by the secretaries, provided with drink, and paraded round for introductions for all the world, Reed said later, as though he were some unique specimen miraculously caught in the nets of matrimony—which perhaps he was. Certainly the young ladies could not have been prouder of him if they were planning to marry him themselves. Kate, meanwhile, accepted a drink from Professor Goddard, the medievalist, who offered congratulations.

"I cannot remember," Kate said, "when I have had so overwhelmingly the sensation of having done something devastatingly clever. As though I had been saved after days in the bottom of a well or lost in the depths of the forest. And yet you know," she added, in a more confidential tone of voice, "Reed and I have known and cared for each other for a long time."

"No matter," Professor Goddard said. "A wedding is destiny, and hanging likewise."

"Did *Piers Plowman* say that?" Kate asked. Kate's total ignorance of *Piers Plowman* was one of her most guilty secrets.

"No. John Heywood; too late to be in my period. But I shall find you a properly dull tag from *Piers Plowman* and have it framed for you both as a wedding present. It may serve, in these days of frantic relevance, to remind you of the importance of the useless."

"The useless is never important, it is only comforting,"

Robert O'Toole said, coming up. "I'm glad you're getting married," he added. "All women should be married. An unmarried woman is an offense against nature." He seemed to find this a marvelously witty remark, despite Kate's look, which indicated clearly to Reed all the way across the room that Kate was finding Robert O'Toole an offense against nature. Kate, who, when she was really offended, had to think with both hands for a fortnight before becoming possessed of a satisfactory retort, was fortunately saved from beginning on this endeavor by the voice of Emilia Airhart, who had joined them. "What I can never understand about you, Mr. O'Toole," she said, "is whether you think arrogant bad manners encourage the illusion of manliness, or whether you think that evident unmanliness is somehow obscured by arrogant bad manners."

Professor Peter Packer Pollinger interrupted whatever response anyone could possibly have found to make to this observation, which was delivered in the voice of one noticing, pleasantly, some mild natural phenomenon, by strolling up to Kate and handing her a book.

"Didn't wrap it," he said. "Many happy weddings."

"Don't you mean many happy returns?" one of the secretaries skittishly asked.

"Mean what I say. She's beginning late, but she may take to it and keep at it, you never know. Here you are, anyway, regardless." Kate was pleased to receive an old book from which all indication of title and author had long since been eradicated by use. She opened therefore to the title page. *The Mountain Lovers*, she read—Fiona Macleod. "Wasn't an easy choice," he said, "for your first wedding. *The Immoral Hour*, *The Divine Adventure*, or even, though I hope not, *The Dominion*, might have done equally well. Have you ever been lovers on a mountain?"

To this embarrassing question, which ought to have

been answered in the affirmative for veracity's sake, in the negative for the sake of everyone's feelings, and for propriety's sake by what her mother used to call a deprecating *moue*, Kate was fortunately saved from responding. (I might, she later observed to Reed, have tried a deprecating *moue* and failed; how awful a thought.) Jeremiah Cudlipp had entered the room, announcing that he had had a terrible day in such stentorian tones that every conversation stopped in deference to him. Kate managed only to take Professor Pollinger's hand and thank him with the affection and gratitude she felt.

The room was now rather full, and almost all of Kate's colleagues had found an opportunity to converse with Reed. As an Assistant D.A. he had no doubt encountered worse ordeals, but this could scarcely be easy, and as Kate regarded the relaxed pose of his long, lanky form from across the room she was suddenly visited with an enormous affection. Odd that she should have to see him in a room full of academics before realizing wherein exactly his unique attraction lay: he was vital without being intense, confident without being assertive, assured without being pompous. She was certain he found this whole phenomenon amusing, and was particularly pleased to see him make his way over to Emilia Airhart—who, naturally, would not want to appear to be looking him over—and engage her in conversation. They appeared to like each other. Into this *tête-à-tête* plunged Jeremiah Cudlipp.

Before Kate could even consider the outcome of such a threesome, Cartier came up to her. He seemed to consider his presence sufficient comment on Kate's marital state, and plunged immediately into questions about University matters, though it was a moment or two before this became wholly clear. "What do you think," he asked, "are the chances for things turning out well? Do you feel doomed to frustration, or slightly optimistic?"

"Well . . ."

"The meeting of the English Department seemed to offer far more hope than I had thought possible; at the same time . . ."

"O'Toole being chosen Dean is not a hopeful sign," Kate said, pulling herself together.

"Most depressing," Cartier said. "Well, cheers," he inconsequentially added, and disappeared as Mark Everglade approached.

"I like your Reed Amhearst," he said. "I thought it only fair to admit that you and I had been stuck in an elevator together in the recent past, and he complimented me on such good company under the circumstances. He's the first lawyer I've ever really cared for, if you want to know. I wonder what the position of the Law School will be on the future of University College."

"I can answer that, I think," Kate said. "They will be for it, partly because they resent The College, which acts as though *it* were the University, but mainly because their secretaries take jobs in order to attend University College free; no University College, no secretaries. The same may be said of the School of Public Administration and probably of several others."

"It really is extraordinary," Everglade said, "the way one works one's ass off for important ideas and principles, only to find that decisions are made in the end for reasons of petty convenience by people who have no more stake in the quality or general movement of education than I have in the changing rate of arbitrage. I don't believe the Trojan War took place over Helen or anyone else. No doubt it began and ended because Hector needed a secretary and Thetis had some sort of working arrangement with Hephaestus about new shields."

"Homer told that story," Kate said. "But if, as Auden has pointed out, Hector or Achilles had written the *Iliad* in the first person, we should have had a comedy, as we have here. Besides, Clio did not love the commanders, the big swaggering figures of history, but those who bred them better horses, found answers to their questions, made their things. If Clio honors anyone, it's us, I think—not mere commanders."

"And Cudlipp is a mere commander?"

"Indubitably. Like boys in pimple-time, like girls at awkward ages, what does he do but wish?"

Everglade smiled. "What do *we* do but wish?" he asked.

The room by now was full to overflowing. Reed and Kate were tall, and their eyes met. Plimsole had caught Michaels in a corner and was making a speech of great length. But for Reed, everyone in the room was tired, wearied with meetings, the extra, unthought-of burdens revolution brings, the sense of impermanence which is perhaps the most wearying of all. For none of them had, previously, questioned the University's power to endure. Certainly one heard of financial crises, community troubles, but for the first time all of them at the University realized that the entire institution might come to grief. Yet, Kate thought, most of the faculty want only to get back to their work—many of them are probably considering offers elsewhere—more money, less turbulence, fewer students. Glancing at Cudlipp, who was now walking toward her, Kate thought of Auden's question: "And how is—what was easy in the past, A democratic villain to be cast?" Stage front and center, Kate thought.

"May I have a word with you, Professor Fansler?" Cudlipp said in his loud, deep voice. Characteristically, he did not wait for an answer. Why are his questions more insulting than other men's assumptions? Kate wondered. "I have had a short talk with Frederick Clemance tonight; he tells me that you two have discussed the future of University College, about which he appears to think there may be some question. He thinks we might at any rate consider the promotion of the two assistant professors we discussed at the recent meeting. I have never heretofore disagreed with Clemance, and I am sorry to do so now. But since you seem to be representing the fight for University College here in the English Department, I thought it only fair to tell you my views. The University College has to go; Bob O'Toole and I have . . ."

"Come now, Jerry," Clemance said. "This is a party for Kate and her charming lawyer, not for the thrashing out of departmental affairs." He placed a hand on Cudlipp's arm.

"I've got a frightful headache," Cudlipp said, acknowledging nothing. He reached into his pocket for a tube of pills, and shook two of them out into his hand.

"I'll get you some club soda to take them with," Clemance said. "You've really got to take it a bit easy, you know." But Cudlipp was gathering his forces. "Look at this catalogue," he began, haranguing Kate as Clemance came up carrying a glass and a bottle of club soda.

"Thank you," Cudlipp said at last when he had gulped the two pills. "I've spent the whole day listening to the representatives from your University College. Four students who appear to be in your class; Dean Frogmore, Bill McQuire from Economics, whom I really would have expected to have more sense; all of them going on as though that silly extension school, degree-granting though it may be, were actually viable, actually . . ."

Cudlipp turned white and apparently grew dizzy, for he reached out to balance himself against one of the desks. "My God," Kate heard him say, "aspirin. Aspirin." And before any one could move at all he had vomited violently, brown blood the color of coffee grounds.

Everyone except Reed was too stunned to move. "Call the hospital," he said to one of the secretaries, who had rushed over, "tell them we have an emergency case, hemorrhaging, blood loss from the stomach. You," he said, pointing to Plimsole, rendered amazingly silent, "help me get him into the elevator. We better not wait for an ambulance. Isn't the hospital right down the street?"

Plimsole helped Reed to lift Cudlipp, no mean weight. With the assistance of two other professors, they were able actually to carry him. Kate ran ahead to ring for the elevator which, for a miracle, was waiting at the eighth floor. She held the doors open as they carried Cudlipp in. While the doors were closing, Kate saw Cudlipp vomit again. Plimsole pressed the button and the elevator started. Everyone stood there, uncertain what to do next. "Perhaps I'd better run down and help them," O'Toole, who had seemed too stunned to move, said. He raced down the stairs, followed by Clemance, who moved more slowly.

But, as it happened, the elevator reached the main floor many minutes after O'Toole and Clemance. It had stuck between the third and fourth floors, Cudlipp had continued vomiting, and by the time they got him out of the elevator and to the hospital it was too late. He had lost great amounts of blood, and they could not revive him. He died that night.

It was almost morning when Kate opened the door to Reed, and for a moment, seeing each other, they remembered the reason for the party that had so abruptly ended and were glad in spite of everything.

But sooner or later they had to talk about it. "It's quite a while," Reed said, "since I watched a man die, though technically he wasn't yet dead when the hospital carted him off. The appalling irony of it is that he had time to call out 'aspirin,' and there were God knows how many people in the room who could interpret that remark—I'll explain it to you in a minute. I knew exactly what to do, we all did exactly the right thing, but the elevator stuck, the mucous membrane of the stomach began to erode very near to a major artery—talk about destiny. He's dead.

How much difference will that make in the whole University picture?"

"I've no idea. Does it really matter?"

"I think it might; I very strongly suspect that he was murdered."

Kate stared at him. "But you've only just now said that given your presence, and lots of other factors, it was really only the most extraordinary bad luck that he died."

"Perhaps you're right. If I decide to run someone over with my car, injuring him sufficiently so that he will be out of commission for a good while, and by mistake I skid and kill him, would you or would you not call it murder?"

"Great Scot," Kate said. She was, when really affected, likely to revert to the innocent ejaculations of her childhood. "What's it all got to do with aspirin?"

"Like many other common medicines, aspirin is a poison to some people."

"I never knew that. Aren't Americans supposed to gulp down millions of aspirin tablets a year?"

"They are not only supposed to; they do. Not to mention the aspirin they swallow in Alka-Seltzer, Coricidin, Pepto Bismol, and fifteen other household remedies you might care to mention. But to some people aspirin is a deadly poison. The moment it is absorbed by the blood stream—and that doesn't take very long, nor, which is more mysterious, does the amount of aspirin taken matter—an allergic person begins to suffer erosion of his mucous membrane. He feels dizzy and weak, he vomits—you saw before you a classic demonstration. There is, I now learn, more and more question whether aspirin ought, in fact, to be as readily available as it is."

"What would they have done if they had got him in the hospital on time?"

"An interesting point we need now never really explore. Probably they would have wasted time doing blood tests, and so forth. They would probably suspect an ulcer or something of the sort. What is of special interest, however, is not only that there probably were many people in that room who knew Cudlipp was allergic to aspirin, but that I am still in the D.A.'s Office and able, therefore, to demand and get a certain amount of prompt action from the hospital. It's almost as though Cudlipp were given the aspirin under conditions guaranteed to prevent a fatality."

"Couldn't he have taken the aspirin by accident? I mean, couldn't it all have been a mistake?"

"Not a bit likely. Someone who knows he's allergic to aspirin—and Cudlipp knew—would have to be forced at gun point to take it. In fact, Cudlipp was in the habit of taking an imported product—made in England. I have it here." Reed put a bottle of pills on the table. "All labeled and clear. An analgesic without aspirin: in other words, a pain-killer which does not expand the blood vessels."

"Paracetamol, B.P." Kate read.

"B.P. is British Pharmaceutical, in case you wondered. I discovered there is an American product, in capsule form, now available, but Cudlipp had supposedly got used to Paracetamol and continued to use it."

"Wouldn't he have tasted the aspirin?"

"What a clever girl you are, to be sure; it took me five hours to think of that question. But I know why you thought of it. What kind of aspirin do you use?"

"The cheapest sort they have in the drugstore. My doctor said aspirin is aspirin and it's preposterous to pay more than a dollar for five hundred of them."

"He's right, of course, except that if you don't happen to like the taste of aspirin, which will begin to dissolve on the tongue immediately, you pay considerably more than that and buy buffered aspirin—you are acquiring, in your new husband, a buffered aspirin eater, by the way—which doesn't taste any more than Paracetamol does; get it?"

"Someone, therefore, supposedly replaced Cudlipp's

Parawhateveritis with a buffered aspirin that looked the same. How much else about you is there that I do not know?"

"I shall refuse to follow that entrancing thought, and plod on instead with the question of aspirin-analgesics. You know, in any case, how dull I am when puzzled."

"I was just thinking earlier this evening how enchanting you are at all times. You know, Reed, I think if you'd only come to a Department party earlier, and let me see you, beautifully lanky and relaxed among all those professors, I would have proposed long ago. Would you have accepted?"

"Probably with a lot less trepidation than I have now. You know, Kate, I've never really minded your being a sort of overage Nancy Drew . . ."

"Now that's unkind, Reed, that's downright nasty . . ."

"Forgive me. I guess I realized you were going to be smack in the middle of this business and I was hoping, in my manly way, that you might be willing to bow out—you know, just go on with what you were doing."

"But none of us can just go on with what we were doing; it's just no longer possible, not, at least, if you're the sort who listens and admits to being confused, which is something no one ever said of Nancy Drew. But why are you getting the wind up so? It's unlike you. I know it's a ghastly mess, but after all, it could have been an accident —or somebody may have put some aspirin in his British thingammies months ago."

"They mightn't, as it happens. Naturally, that's the first thing I looked into. He was beginning on a new load of pills just today—yesterday, I guess, by now—and the entire bottle of two hundred tablets is O.K., so clearly, it was the small tube in which he carried a day's supply of pills around with him that had been tampered with. As it happens, the two he took at the party were the first of the new batch, but he might have taken them at any time—he was nervous, and prone to headaches. Someone got hold of that pill-carrier, supposedly after Cudlipp had filled it, and replaced the first two British pills with buffered aspirin."

"There, you see," Kate said. "And he might have taken them anywhere, and I wouldn't have been at all involved."

"You weren't near his office that day, no. But you had had lunch with Clemance some days before—though you had admired the man this side of idolatry for decades without finding it necessary to lunch with him before. And, as it happened, Cudlipp was talking to you when he decided to take the pills, and Clemance rushed right off and got him some soda water—right?"

"Right. Who noticed that?"

"Just about everyone."

"Well, all it proves is that I couldn't have had anything to do with it. If he had just got the new pills today, I wouldn't have had time to substitute the aspirin for the pills in his pill tube."

"You could have done it right at the party."

"My dear man, I may be Nancy Drew; I'm not Houdini."

"The fact is, anyone at the party could have done it. He carried the tube with the pills loose in his outer pocket; child's play. Or anyone who visited his office today—which includes students from your beloved University College (which should have gone right on being extension courses, if you want my candid opinion), Frogmore, McQuire, and one or two other chaps from that little luncheon you had before you asked me to marry you."

"Reed, aren't you being a little over-dramatic? If any-one wanted to kill Cudlipp in that way, doesn't it seem likely that it was someone of a non-university sort? His wife, someone like that?"

"When you hear the history of the pills, I think you'll discount that."

"*Is* Cudlipp married?"

"He and his wife have recently separated, amidst much acrimony, I am given to understand."

"You've picked up more in five hours than I have in five years."

"You are not, I am pleased to say, a gossipy sort. What floors, by the way, were you stuck between when you and Everglade were in that elevator together?"

Kate stared at him. "The third and fourth. Why?"

Reed took her in his arms. "Why indeed?" he said. And then for a while forgot all about it.

CHAPTER SEVEN

Between those happenings that prefigure it
And those that happen in its anamnesis
Occurs the Event, but that no human wit
Can recognize until all happening ceases.

"To put it crudely," Frogmore said, "Cudlipp's death can be the end for us, or the beginning. I would not have lifted a finger to injure Cudlipp, but if his death can help the University College, I will make use of it. Need I say more?"

"It will scarcely help us," McQuire remarked, "to have the University College discovered to be the motive for the murder. It does seem to suggest that we don't produce people of the right sort. There is, after all, a distinction between occupying the President's Office and murder. Or so I assume."

"Correctly, I am certain," Hankster said in his hoarse whisper.

The same group who had met previously, when McQuire had brought Kate to luncheon, was now reconvened, minus the student (to Kate's relief). She did not doubt the judgment of students, which, in some cases, she valued over that of the faculty, but she did doubt their discretion. In a case like this, rumor could do irreparable harm, particularly if it were true.

Castleman apparently not only understood the power structure of the University with remarkable clarity but with ease shifted this understanding to problems of murder. "We have donned our academic gowns and attended a memorial service for Cudlipp," he said, "and we have all contributed to a fund to establish a prize in his honor."

"To be awarded, naturally, to an outstanding student in the College," Frogmore said.

"Naturally," Castleman acknowledged. "But we had better realize that the administration and the senior faculty are profoundly shaken by all this. Disruption is one thing, murder—however haphazard in appearance—another. It follows inevitably that if Cudlipp was given the aspirin accidentally, more or less at random as a flying brick may hit *someone*, that is one thing; if he was given the aspirin intentionally as part of some personal grudge or individual pottiness, that is another. If, however, he was poisoned fatally on behalf of any school in this University, or any group of students or faculty . . ." Castleman shrugged, not bothering to complete his sentence.

"Whether fortunately or not," McQuire said, "we know exactly when Cudlipp got this latest batch of non-aspirins, so we know that the substitution of the pills must have taken place on that day, the day of Kate's party."

"I don't see how that really helps us," Cartier said.

"It helps the detective work, not us," Castleman pointed out. "It means that the aspirin Cudlipp took had to be given to him that day—they couldn't have been mixed in with his British pills, simply waiting for him to light on them. We know, furthermore, whom Cudlipp saw that day. Alas, having refused for weeks to talk to anyone from the University College, he appears, on the day of his death, to have decided to lend his ear if not his sympathy."

"That may have been thanks to Clemance," Kate said.

"Thanks are not, as it has turned out, what we especially want to offer," Frogmore said.

"That's unfair, I think," Kate said.

"Of course it is," Frogmore agreed.

"We know," Castleman went on, "that on the afternoon

of the day of his death, Cudlipp saw McQuire and Frogmore and Cartier; he agreed to be called upon by four students from the University College; he also had a conference about the College English Department with Clemance and O'Toole. In the morning he had a class; he had lunch with Hankster and . . ."

"And," Hankster added, "we were joined by Professor Emilia Airhart."

"Which does not, of course," Kate added, "necessarily account for everyone he saw that day. There are the secretaries, casual encounters on campus paths . . ."

"And in the men's room," Hankster said. "Let's face it, anyone could have switched those pills, if murder were the intent. I don't believe it was. I think someone copped what he thought were a couple of aspirins, and then returned others, unaware of their lethal qualities for Cudlipp."

"Then," Castleman said, "we've got to find him—the innocent aspirin-changer."

"Perhaps he will confess," Frogmore said. "Let us hope so. Meanwhile, I would like to know what the next move is—for University College. Whether or not we can find the person who caused Cudlipp's death, we can certainly determine the effect of the death on us. O'Toole will be taken up with running the College. Clemance, while not our advocate, seems actually to have some decent sense of reticence about wiping us off the face of the map. The Graduate English Department, from what I can gather, is all for promoting our assistant professors from the English Department, helping themselves and doing the College in the eye at the same time. I think we ought to move."

"Move cautiously," Castleman said, "but move—I agree with you. Let's discover, in an informal way, how the administration feels."

"I thought we were clean out of administration," Kate said.

"The Administrative Council is still functioning," Frogmore said, "and will go on until we get the Senate. The Acting President has promised that a statement of confidence in the viability of University College, and instructions to departments to promote its qualified faculty to tenure, will come before the next meeting of the Administrative Council."

"Which is when?" Hankster asked.

"In three weeks, and every hour of that time has to be used to get us the votes we need—not only in favor of the motion, but also against a motion to table for any reason whatsoever—for example, so that all undergraduate education at the University can be studied. Because if the Administrative Council doesn't give us its mandate we're as good as finished. By the time we get a Senate and a new President it will be a whole new ball game—as Cudlipp knew."

"So his being out of the picture will make a difference?"

"Oh, yes," Frogmore said, "all the difference in the world. Cudlipp had a lot of favors to trade, and now isn't around to trade them."

Kate walked from the meeting with Hankster; she fell in step beside him so that, without being rude, he had no choice but to proceed at her side—and Hankster was never rude. He had, since the spring, acquired a reputation for devoted, radicalism; yet, *tête-à-tête* with him, one found it hard to believe. Not only the scarcely audible voice—the intimation was that he was unable to speak loudly, though Kate suspected strategic rather than physical inhibitions—belied the drama of radicalism. He was a gentleman, from the top of his sleek head, past the elegant clothes, to the tips of his beautifully made shoes. Kate, because she had come from his world, understood him, and knew better than most that there are those who cling to the finger bowls, those who dismiss them with a shrug but not without nostalgia, and those like Hankster whose life was devoted to smashing the finger bowls against privy walls.

"What did you talk about with Cudlipp, if I may be forthright enough to ask? If you don't want to tell me, don't; spare me the gentlemanly circumlocutions."

"I'm honored," Hankster said. "As I have gathered, you're often peppery, but seldom rude. You dislike me very much, don't you?"

Kate stopped a moment, with Hankster waiting patiently by her side. "Yes," Kate said, "I do. I think I always dislike people who are destroyers by principle, though I never really faced up to it, until this moment. Sorry. I've no right to ask you any questions at all."

"Sure you have. You really think, don't you, that we've seen the last of the troubles. That from now on, we just rebuild our university, better than before but not fundamentally different."

"Oh, I expect students will sit in buildings, or whatever the new ploy is, again this spring. But I don't think it will make any real difference; not here. We've had our moment of awakening. This spring, it will be other universities who have the uprisings; don't you agree?"

"Perhaps. But the whole system's finished all the same. Sure, you'll have your Senate, which will bring students and junior faculty into the system, and will perhaps keep an antediluvian administration from making the kinds of mistakes which, in any case, they aren't going to make anymore, because no university will ever again have so basically stupid a president as this university had. But it's only reaction you're institutionalizing. Administrators on the whole, you know, are more up-to-date than the senior faculty. That's where the bastion of conservatism is, if you want to know. And this Senate will simply give them more power. So—when the big break comes, it will be a lulu."

"And you look forward to it, hope for it, will work for it?"

"It will happen whatever I do, though I'll lend a hand if I can. I don't know what revolutions you're dreaming of, Professor Fansler, or hoping for, or fearing."

Kate laughed. "You're accusing me, in your ever-polite way, of being like the dreaming lady in an anecdote of Kenneth Burke's. She dreamed a brute of a man had entered her bedroom and was staring at her from the foot of her bed. 'Oh, what are you going to do to me?' she asked, trembling. 'I don't know, lady,' the brute answered; 'it's your dream.' "

Hankster laughed. "It is delightful to talk to someone who enjoys one's point, even against herself."

"I know. It's our guilts and our hidden desires that you work on most, you radicals. We shall destroy ourselves in the end, whether because we understand the radical students too well or too little."

"But it's not just the radical students; it's all students. There simply is no longer any reason for their being in college—not the smart ones, anyway. The engineering students, those on their way up the social ladder, the blacks —college has some point for them. But for the bright kid who's been to a first-rate high school, what's he got to learn at college? He no longer comes to college for his first drink, his first woman. Until college becomes a privilege again. . . ."

"But that's the point of the University College—for the older students. Education is again something they've had to earn."

"The University College, and places like it, are the future. Whether this University has the sense to see that or not is important only to us here, now, but in the end it will make no difference. The question is not *if* the state will take over this University, but when. Every year, also, fewer kids make it through undergraduate education uninterrupted. To leave college is the norm, not the exception now. The whole picture's changing. That, if you want to know, is what I talked to Cudlipp about at lunch. Since I teach in both the adult and the boys' colleges, he wanted to know where my loyalties lay."

"And what did you tell him?" Kate asked.

"That I was a smasher of finger bowls. But ask your colleague Emilia Airhart. She joined us near the beginning."

"How come?"

"I met her and asked her to."

"Didn't Cudlipp mind?"

"Horribly. He dislikes women if they are not beautiful, not slender, not stupider than he—or willing to pretend they are—and not flirtatious. Mrs. Airhart made a clean sweep. You would do better, or would have done; we will never know now."

"I am quite past deciding if that is nasty or nice. Anyway, I like Emilia Airhart."

"So do I. And if you ask her, she will tell you that Cudlipp tried to co-opt me and I said no. The system's finished. You and I came out of the same world, but only one of us dreams of going back."

"I know I can't go back," Kate said. "I just don't hate the memory. What's Frogmore going to do now?"

"What everyone must do: reach every member of the Administrative Council; tell each one a vote for University College is a vote against the growing power mania of *The* College. We'll come through now. It's truly amazing what aspirin can cure, wouldn't you say?"

Kate found Emilia Airhart in her office riffling, as one seemed to do these days, through mimeographed pages. "Come in," she called to Kate. "I was just about to write you a note. One less dirty piece of paper, thank God. I knew I had lost my interest in revolution when I lost my interest in mimeographed announcements from every splinter group on campus demanding this, foretelling that, condemning the other. There is now even an organization for liberating women—utter nonsense. Women are liberated the moment they stop caring what other women think of them." With a gesture of great delight she dumped the whole package of papers into the waste basket. "I hear you're an admirer of Auden's and have just sponsored a brilliant dissertation on him."

"Yes, though the less said about the dissertation defense, the better. There was a moment there when I feared for the whole future of the academic world."

"Do tell. Professor Pollinger mentioned it as the most interesting dissertation defense he had been to in years. What *do* you admire about Auden, by the way, if you can enunciate it in several well-chosen sentences—a talent of yours, I'm told."

"I can't imagine by whom. As a matter of fact, I babble on, hitting the truth occasionally by happenstance which inspires students by the sheer surprise of it; the rest of the time they just feel comfortably superior. As to Auden, he's interested in squares and oblongs, rather than in sensory effects, which I like; that is, he understands that men always have moral dilemmas, which makes him intelligent, and he is able to present these structurally, which makes him an artist. The structures he uses are patterns of words, which make him a poet. He's conceptual rather than descriptive, and he always sees objects, natural or not, as part of a relationship. He knows that, first and last, a poet has to express abstract ideas in concrete forms, his own words, as it happens. How's that for a one-minute lecture?"

"Brilliant."

"Thank you. I stole it from Richard Hoggart's introduction to Auden's poems, which Mr. Cornford in turn quoted in his dissertation. If you want to know what I personally admire, well Auden knows that poetry 'makes nothing happen,' though it is of supreme importance: the only order. And Auden is the only poet I know whose poems are serious and *fun*. He refuses to let poetry be pompous *or* empty. That's why he appreciates Clio, and leaves the other muses alone. Clio 'looks like any girl one has not noticed,'

> Muse of the unique
> Historical fact, defending with silence
> Some world of your beholding, a silence
>
> No explosion can conquer but a lover's Yes
> Has been known to fill. . . .

Think of that in connection with Cudlipp for example. An explosion of sorts conquered him, but can you think of him as filled by a lover's Yes?"

"Now that you mention it, no. He was always empty and scorned girls one had not noticed. I'm wondering, actually, about the plays Auden wrote with Isherwood."

"Must you?"

"Duty calls. A student wants to work on them, and who am I to say him nay? Will you kind of advise on the Auden part?"

"All right. But I don't look forward to the dissertation defense."

"Our examinations are all wrong. In Sweden, the whole thing is done what I call properly. There's a professor who attacks the work, a professor who defends it, and a third who makes humorous remarks, which of course we're all dying to do but never can do properly in this country. Then when it's over the candidate gives a ball, white tie and long dresses. I'm thinking of emigrating."

"It's true," Kate said. "When formality went from life, meaning went too. People always yowl about form without meaning, but what turns out to be impossible is mean-

ing without form. Which is why I'm a teacher of literature
and keep ranting on about structure. Perhaps it's different
in the drama."

"On the contrary. When a culture no longer agrees on
form, it loses drama. Certain ardent souls, to be sure, try
to get effects by undressing on the stage, having inter-
course in front of the audience, perhaps even getting the
audience to join them, but it won't work. That's why
films are the thing today—perceived in loneliness, like
novels."

"I thought the young were all mad for film-making
today—quite ritualistic and groupy."

"Making them, perhaps. But one *sees* a film in the dark,
alone. Isherwood and Auden plays, though, could count
on an audience of the left."

"Sure—like today. The bad guys were in, and the good
guys wanted to get them out. Things were simpler then,
though. I have often wished I were not among the
Epigoni:

No good expecting long-legged ancestors to
Return with long swords from pelagic paradises. . . .
Meanwhile, how should a cultured gentleman behave?

Which reminds me, what about your lunch with Hankster and Cudlipp?"

"Well, Cudlipp disliked me, and Hankster disliked
Cudlipp and wanted to make him uncomfortable. It was
one of those situations no one could get out of without
being brutal, and so far one doesn't openly snub a colleague in the Faculty Club. In short, Cudlipp wanted
Hankster to admit he was a gentleman and come in with
the College in some grand though unspecified position;
Hankster declined."

"Was Hankster alone with Cudlipp at all in the Club
that day?"

"They were at a table together before I came—not for long, I think. They were together in the men's room, one supposes; I was in the ladies' room and can't be sure. I was alone with Cudlipp for a minute; I ought to tell you that. Hankster got up in search of a bottle of ale, the waiter having apparently gone on some extended errand in another part of the forest, you know how it is in the Faculty Club. When are you getting married?"

"I don't know. Reed says we'll talk about it tonight, if we can get our minds off Cudlipp's aspirin. Emilia, did Cudlipp ever promise you anything to get your support for the College?"

"Yes. He promised me positions for women in the College, which he thought dear to my heart. What does it matter now? Anyway, why shouldn't you have your University College? A new experience, like getting married."

"I hadn't looked at it in that light. It really represents new experiences for everyone."

"Essential to a well-lived life. Take loneliness, for instance. Terrible in its way. And yet, for me, a few days of complete solitude in the country, away from an outrageously happy marriage, work I love, and noisy, gifted children is a joy so intense that perhaps not even Auden could describe it. But one day too much, and one plunges into the abyss of enforced solitude, of not being wanted or missed. I don't know if you or Auden ever noticed it, but the only earthly joys are those we are free to choose— like solitude, your college, certain marriages."

"And what about unearthly joys?"

"Ah, those, if we are fortunate, choose us. Like grace. Like talent."

Mark Everglade caught Kate as she emerged into the hall. "Just the person I wanted to see. We shall want your advice. We haven't done too well with Swahili, but we're interviewing someone who reads and writes Ndebele. You needn't look blank; as everyone should know these days, that's a dialect of Zulu, and contains the greatest literature of Africa not in English. We're stirring up people to come and chat with him tomorrow between two and four. Do try to come."

"But what on earth will I talk to him about?"

"Offer to help him translate the novels of Bulwer-Lytton into Ndebele. A way of preparing for next year's text course."

"But why do we have to teach Ndebele literature in the English Department?"

"The Elephant's Child," Mark Everglade said. "There you go again. We are restructuring after the revolution, remember?" And Kate, remembering, went off to teach her class in Victorian literature.

She returned home somewhat late that afternoon, showered, dressed, and went to meet Reed at his apartment where, he had announced, he was preparing dinner. "My plan is this," he had said. "If we are going to get married, there are bound to be evenings when we will not feel like eating out. There is a place which, with ample notice and heroic payment, will send up some sort of casserole all ready to be popped into the oven, but the way I figure it, once or twice a week we will want to eat in and *cook*. I know you can cook at least three dishes, because I've eaten them, and I've just learned from a friend that if you have a fireplace like mine you can buy little thingamajigs with which to make logs out of *The New York Times* (I'm getting quite the married man, you see, finding a use for everything), and then we can grill steaks over an open fire, but I still ought to be able to make a contribution. I have therefore learned to cook one dish and will soon learn to cook another, both in an electric frying pan which a bachelor friend of mine gave me. (I took that, by the way, as a sure sign that I ought to get married.) You are to come and eat sausages and peppers with crisp bread, cucumber sticks sprinkled with fresh-ground pepper, red wine, and black coffee. I've discovered that to appear a gourmet, one serves too little food, highly seasoned: the sausages are hot."

He greeted Kate with a book in hand. "Here," he said, "listen to this; it should make anything delectable." The book was *Letters from Iceland*, and Reed read from Auden's tourist guide: " 'Dried fish is a staple food in Iceland. This should be shredded with the fingers and eaten with butter. It varies in toughness. The tougher kind tastes like toe-nails, and the soft kind like the skin off the soles of one's feet.' Bound to make peppers and sausage luscious, don't you agree? Sit down and let me fix you a drink. Then I'll give you my news."

"Here's a passage you missed," Kate said, reading from the book. " 'A curious Icelandic food,' he says, 'is Hakarl, which is half-dry, half-rotten shark. This is white inside with a prickly horn rind outside, as tough as an old boot.' Auden seems to have become a foot fetishist in Iceland. 'Owing to the smell it has to be eaten out of doors. It is shaved off with a knife and eaten with brandy.' Do you think he can be serious? 'It tastes more like boot polish than anything else I can think of.' I'm not at all certain," Kate said, accepting her drink from Reed, "that I want to eat at all."

"When you hear my news you'll want to eat even less. I have had visitors from your glorious University, not to say from one of your select, conspiratorial lunches. Marrying you makes for a busy life, that much is clear."

"Frogmore and McQuire, by any chance?"

"Castleman and Klein. Castleman, it turns out, knows some of my associates, and Klein knows others, so they decided to trust me. They were further encouraged in this decision by the fact that I was present when Cudlipp took the aspirin, and as helpful as possible when he died, which isn't saying much. They were very kind, formal, discrete, and honorable, and I didn't envy them their mission at all."

"Reed! They came to ask you to be President of the University! You've no idea the trouble everyone's having finding presidents these days. Who wants the job? It was bad enough when one had to raise money and talk to rich alumni, but these, however stupid and trying, never occupied one's office or ransacked one's files. I hope you turned them down flat."

"They came to ask if I thought you had interpreted their plea for help at luncheon and Frogmore's enthusiasm for his school as a mandate to put Cudlipp out of commission. Their motive in inquiring, I gathered, was not law and order but simple clarity: they wanted to ascertain who had slipped Cudlipp the aspirin in a wholly admirable effort to establish who had *not*."

"But why on earth me? I didn't even know about Cudlipp's blasted British pills, I haven't that sort of mind, and while I have admittedly become devoted to the cause of the University College, there are limits to my devotion even to so worthy a cause. Do you think it's blackmail?"

"By God, Kate, for the first time I have come to appreciate your blasted revolution. Such sangfroid well becomes you. I remember once, years ago, having to tell you that you were suspected of murder and you burst into tears and had to be comforted with pats on the head and hot coffee."

"What a long memory you have."

"It didn't have to be all that long to enable me to recall that you were standing with Cudlipp when he took the aspirin. In fact, he was arguing with you at the time."

"Arguing is a bit strong—for Cudlipp, who never did anything else. I'm sure he was bald because he'd torn out his hair so often it decided to give up the struggle. He was wielding the University College catalogue, as a matter of fact, presumably prior to letting me know how inferior the offerings were—or am I theorizing ahead of my data?"

"Since, short of séances, that's as much data on Cudlipp's intentions as we're likely to have—no."

"What else, if anything, did Castleman and Klein want —after you convinced them that I was Nancy Drew and not Lucretia Borgia?"

"They wanted to know if I'd help."

"Clever of them; but didn't they guess I'd have asked you already?"

"Their asking me made it semi-official."

"Like our relationship now. I can hardly wait for Thanksgiving."

"Thanksgiving is only four weeks away."

"Reed, that is the most ungallant remark you have ever made, and that's saying a good deal. I know I said you couldn't back out after the secretaries' party, but after all, we hardly expected Cudlipp to pop off like that, so you can always say there were extenuating circumstances. Only be kind enough to remember that *I* only asked to move in with you and have you cook sausages and peppers in your new electric frying pan; *I* never asked for legal assurances."

"Kate darling, that was not a remark, it was an observation, and the 'only' referred not to my implied regrets about my waning days of bachelorhood, but to the fact that the meeting of the Administrative Council which is to decide the fate of University College is scheduled for one week before Thanksgiving. As Castleman and Klein point out, if the question of Cudlipp's death isn't closed by then, the matter of the University College may be. It is being widely suggested to the Board of Governors, the administration, and everyone else in sight that no move should be taken in the matter while any suspicions about Cudlipp's death remain. Castleman's sense of things is that if approval doesn't come at the next meeting, it will likely never come at all. In fact he quoted the line about a tide in the affairs of men and so forth. Cudlipp's death has got to be cleared up a week before the four weeks to Thanksgiving—hence my unfortunate observation."

"Well, I'm mollified if not reassured. Are you supposed to deliver the murderer's head on a platter—that is, with enough evidence to prosecute—or is the Board of Governors' knowledge of what happened sufficient?"

"It's not only sufficient, it's advisable. After all, the chances are still open that it was all an accident. Castleman and Klein, who are men of real substance, want to be able to give their word to the Board that the accident was *not* the work of anyone from University College. Then, supposedly, the Administrative Council will proceed. I gather the Board never overrides the Administrative Council."

"They never have, no. And of course once the new Faculty Senate is in business, which should be by the New Year, the Administrative Council will dissolve itself. I agree with Castleman about the tide."

"I didn't actually give Castleman an answer; I said I wanted to talk to you first. I hope I did assure them that not only were you wholly incapable of carrying out such a plot, you were even not likely to have thought of it, among other reasons because, as I would be prepared to swear, you had never heard of the deleterious effects of aspirin until I pointed them out to you. Do you think I ought to help? It's all right with the D.A., by the way, who turns out to be a friend of someone or other."

"Of course you should help. Wasn't that your first impulse?"

"My first impulses, like most people's, are generous. That's why Talleyrand told his ministers to resist first impulses. Not, however, being involved in the French government, I may decide to indulge myself. What fascinates me, you know, is the fact that the aspirin had to be substituted that day. It's impossible that someone had, from whatever motives, dropped two aspirins into his supply at a previous time. That means we can really concentrate on the people Cudlipp saw that day, and we've got his day pretty well covered. That he happened to have spent it almost exclusively in the company of people from the University College is certainly unfortunate."

"Didn't he see anyone else?"

"Clemance and O'Toole. What with the revisions in the College English Department and everywhere else—I will say for you academic people, once you start revising you really make a job of it—he was seeing both of them fairly regularly. With O'Toole about to be Dean, they had plenty to talk about."

"Who'll be chairman of the College English Department now? It's been Cudlipp for years and years, and O'Toole was the heir apparent."

"An interesting question. Do you think you could find out?"

"You're not suggesting someone bumped him off to get the job? I do assure you, Reed, except for Cudlipp, who was power-mad, no one takes the job except as a service to mankind. Look at poor Michaels and Everglade in the Graduate English Department; nothing short of an elephantine sense of duty could have persuaded *them*."

"Perhaps. Haven't you some brilliant ex-student now teaching in the College who would be pleased to visit you and spill the beans?"

"I might. You realize, of course, that almost anyone might have dropped into Cudlipp's office and diddled with his pills. English Department offices are very milling-about sorts of places."

"I know. That's why I shall begin with the Department secretaries. Now let's see. We've got McQuire, Frogmore, and Cartier, each of whom saw Cudlipp in his office, by appointment, on the day he died. Then there are your four students; you might, simply oozing tact and discretion, get them to tell you about their conversation."

"Reed, you know perfectly well I never ooze tact, and will either ask them flatly what happened or not mess with it."

"There is tact and tact. Very well, I'll take on the students. Then there's Hankster and your Mrs. Airhart. Anything likely there?"

"I wouldn't put much past Hankster. But how could he have replaced the top two pills at lunch without Cudlipp noticing? Reed, wait a minute, I've got an idea. Suppose at lunch Cudlipp takes two of his British pills, which are, of course, harmless, and says something to Hankster about them—take these instead of aspirin, ha, ha, or something —and Hankster asks to see the tube, and replaces the top two pills with two aspirin."

"Which he just happened to have on him?"

"Why not? Anyhow, we'll never know now, since he won't have them on him anymore. Maybe that's the whole solution."

"Mrs. Airhart also had lunch with them. Castleman told me. Wouldn't she have seen them diddling with the pills?"

"It would have been before she joined them; in fact, Hankster probably asked her so that he would have a witness for most of the lunch."

"For that matter, Emilia Airhart could have done the same trick with the pills."

"True. She told me she was alone with Cudlipp while Hankster went for an ale. But he probably just went to cast suspicion on her. I *like* Emilia."

"I too like Emilia. I like everybody concerned except the victim."

"Could the victim's estranged wife have sent round doctored pills—suppose she put two regular aspirin in and Cudlipp got them at the first shot?"

"Even if he managed to get one aspirin at the first shot, his chance of getting both was, statistically speaking, non-existent. If we're going to have to count on a long shot like that we'd better give up before we start."

"Speaking of starting, whatever is happening to your sausage and peppers? Don't you think . . ."

"No," Reed said, "I don't. The great thing about electric frying pans, my bachelor friend said, is that they can be ignored for hours and hours."

CHAPTER
EIGHT

but we, at haphazard
And unseasonably, are brought face to face
By ones, Clio, with your silence. . . .
your silence already is there
Between us and any magical center
Where things are taken in hand.

The next morning Kate was able to reach on the telephone a young man presently teaching at the College whose dissertation she was directing. He had been a member of her Victorian Seminar several years back and had, after one-and-a-half semesters of the soundest work on the Corn Laws, Reform Bill, Carlyle, and John Stuart Mill, developed a frivolous and unaccountable passion for Max Beerbohm: not his life, nor his times, nor even his works as such, but his sentences. Since it is impossible to study all of a writer's sentences in the ordinary way without a century of time, the young man (whose name was Higgenbothom, but whom Kate always thought of as Enoch Soames) had soon entangled himself with computers. With something between relief and dismay, Kate had handed him over to a stylistics expert, though she had remained on the dissertation committee. Higgenbothom agreed to come and see her at four, relieved and mystified to learn that his dissertation would not be the subject under discussion.

Having arranged that matter, Kate settled down to the

reading of some student papers, and was soon lost in wonder at the inability of highly intelligent students properly
to construct a sentence. It occurred to her to wonder if
computers might be enlisted in her constant struggle
against wobbly syntax and sociological jargon. "Being a
young writer, the novel was filled with fresh ideas," was
typical of sentences which greeted Kate's wondering eyes.
Nor was this the worst. She read with horror of the sub-
dued dynamics of Ruskin's interpersonal relations and
could not at once hit upon a comment for the margin
which was both succinct and mentionable in a scholarly
ambience. Thinking of Max Beerbohm and then of her
bright, reform-minded young students, Kate marveled not
for the first time at the inverse correlation between moral
outrage and sentence structure: apparently one could be
radical or syntactical but not both; a disturbing thought.
And where, Kate thought, her mind dwelling on interpersonal relations, would Reed have got in his investigations?

Reed, at that moment, was vamping the secretary of
the College English Department, a pitifully easy thing to
do. He had been considering, on the subway, alternate
possible approaches to a subject which, simply stated, was
a demand to be told when Cudlipp received the bottle of
pills, and where and how and what he did with them. The
question was how to counter the inevitable "Who are
you and why do you want to know?" which, while easily
answered in a way, would immediately put the lady on
her guard and negate the possibility of always-useful gossip. As it turned out, he need not have concerned himself.
Miss Elton was a type with which he was agonizingly
familiar. She appeared to have been born with a smirk on
her face; she was one of those whose chief reward in life
lies in snubbing others, particularly women. But let any
male treat her in a truly manly fashion—that is, combining
the worst features of a spoiled teenager and an aging *roué*

—and she would bat her eyelashes as readily as their great load of mascara allowed, and succumb. Before you could say Blazes Boylan, Reed was sitting on the edge of her desk discussing bottles of pills. Auden of course, Reed thought, had got it perfectly:

> *So pocket your fifty sonnets, Bud;*
> *tell Her a myth*
> *Of unpunishable gods and all the girls*
> *they interfered with.*

"He and his wife had separated," Miss Elton confided. "I know because I filled out the application for him to the University housing office; he wanted a small apartment for just him, with a room for the kids to stay once in a while. But the pills were delivered as usual to his regular apartment, and his wife dropped them off here the morning he died. I took them into his office, and he said 'Thank God, I just took the last two,' and he showed me that little gidget he always carried them in was empty. He began opening the bottle, which always made him swear because it was sealed—like whiskey you know—and then he started telling me all the things I had to do while he filled the tube with the pills."

"What things?"

"Well, I'd made the appointments the day before with those jerks from the University College—Cudlipp couldn't stand them, but for some reason he decided to see them; we all supposed Clemance had talked him into it. I heard Cudlipp talking to Clemance recently when they walked out of here and Cudlipp said, 'All right, I'll see those students, but if one of them tries to pressure me, I'll throw him out.' He used to, you know."

Reed raised his eyebrows provocatively.

"Throw people out," she said, giggling. "He would open the door and yell 'Get out!' and if they didn't, he'd put his hands on their chests and push. With men of course. He didn't see women much in his office."

"Was there any chance he would have considered hiring women teachers in the College?" Reed asked, remembering what Emilia Airhart had told Kate.

"I hope not. What a dreary bunch *they* are, all brains and messy hair. The College boys wouldn't go for that, believe me. If we ever get women working around here, I quit; I'd never work for a woman."

"Did all the people Cudlipp had appointments with come to his office or did he go to theirs?"

"You a detective or something?"

"As a matter of fact, I am, but keep it secret, honey. It'll be a real feather in my cap if I can clear things up—you know, universities don't like hanky-panky."

"You ever been a spy?"

"I go where the money is, so long as there's plenty of it. So all of Cudlipp's appointments came here?"

"Yeh. Here's the appointment sheet, Mr. Bond. Though really, I ought to turn my back so you could steal the page underneath the one I wrote the appointments on—the one with the impressions of the writing."

"I'd rather have the writing and impressions of you. Did they all show up on time?" Reed asked, reading the list.

"More or less. He'd allotted half an hour for those students, but he threw them out after fifteen minutes, so he saw Clemance and O'Toole earlier than is down there. I called them and said he was ready. So in they came and shouted a lot, but I couldn't hear about what. Academic stuff, anyhow."

"Do you mean he put his hands on the chests of the students and pushed?"

"One of the men. 'Get out!' he screamed, 'and stay out. Go back to that half-baked school you come from.' "

"Some language from an English professor."

"Yeh. Then he lowered his voice real low and said,

'Miss Elton, tell Mr. Clemance I'm free now.'" Reed had heard Cudlipp only once, but the imitation seemed to him not bad.

"Who do you suppose will be in charge of things around here now?"

"Search me. Of course, there's a new piece of inside dope every other minute, but I figure I'll wait and see. If I don't like the guy, I'll split. There are plenty of jobs."

"There must be lots of high-paying jobs for an efficient, attractive girl like you. Why work in a college where they pay less than a business does?"

"I like being around literary types—I like an intellectual atmosphere. And the young English professors are real brainy and cute."

"Like Robert O'Toole?"

"He's not young—he's a full professor—and what a stuffed shirt! Thinks he's a big deal. Mr. Know-it-all. Tries to imitate Clemance. Now there's a nice old man, really dignified and cool. Always calls me *Miss* Elton. But he's fading away."

"Clemance? He can't be that old, surely. Barely sixty."

"That's ancient. I feel sorry for the old coot. His days of greatness are behind him."

"Sic transit etcetera. Tell me, Miss Elton . . ."

"Jennifer."

"Jennifer. Did Cudlipp ever go to the men's room, or to someone else's office, and leave his tube of pills on his desk?"

"Look, sweetie, I'm the secretary here, not anyone's valet. Your guess is as good as mine."

"Well, thanks, Jennifer; see you around."

"Anytime, poopsie. Take it easy."

Reed waved to the other secretaries in the office who apparently typed for the lower ranks. It had been clear to him early on that Cudlipp and the other full professors in the English Department here were Jennifer Elton's property and none of theirs, so he did not stop to question them. Well, Reed thought, consulting Cudlipp's appointment sheet, here I go. And he headed across the campus to the building that housed the University College and Dean Frogmore.

To Reed's mild surprise, Frogmore agreed to see him almost immediately. Apparently Castleman had cleared the ground.

"Come in, Mr. Amhearst. Please, don't apologize. As a matter of fact, you give me the perfect excuse to get out of a rather boring meeting. I do hope we can settle this Cudlipp business—it's very disturbing, you know."

"Helpful, too, is it not, Dean Frogmore? Speaking frankly."

"It could be very helpful, if we're to be allowed to make use of it. Cudlipp had a great deal of direct power—and he liked to wield it. He was damn clever in the personal deals he made, and he was absolutely set on destroying University College; it was an obsession. Some of the students went to see him, you know, the same day I did, thinking to tell him how great this place is, and he literally threw them out of his office. Frankly, if I'd heard Peabody had hit Cudlipp over the head with a bat, I would have been grieved but not surprised. I'm sure I don't need to mention that Peabody didn't even know about this aspirin business."

"Is there any chance I could talk to Peabody, do you think?"

"I'll do the best I can for you; hold on a minute." Frogmore went over and stuck his head out the door: "Miss Philips, would you see if you can locate John Peabody? And let me know when you do. It's rather important. Thank you." He shut the door and returned to his desk. Academic secretaries, Reed observed, were cherished; they were not issued orders over the telephone.

"Had you heard," Reed asked, "that Cudlipp had

attended the University College during his own under-graduate days?"

"I had heard, and it's quite true, interestingly enough. This place was called the extension school then, and it had even less prestige, university-wise, than it has now." (Reed wondered if Frogmore had used "university-wise" to Kate, who hated the word formation. "Do you know what the mama owl said to the papa owl?" Kate would ask; "How's the baby wisewise?" The only harsh criticism she had ever been known to make of Auden had been on this score: "something odd was happening soundwise," he had, unforgivably, written in a poem.) "I guess it's the typical syndrome," Frogmore said, blissfully unaware of his offense. "Cudlipp, we now know, was simply incapable of any objectivity on the question of University College. And, of course, he managed to carry the College faculty and alumni with him."

"Of course. Snobbism transforms itself into intelligent discrimination when practiced by ordinarily rational people."

"That's nice, Mr. Amhearst. I like that. You've heard that we began by trying to convince them that we were good—and then one day at luncheon Professors Castle-man and Klein, whom you've met, told us we had to begin to attack politically. We did begin—with the Grad-uate English Department; and we were doing very well when this happened. "Don't misunderstand me, Mr. Am-hearst. With Cudlipp out of the way we have a much better chance. But O'Toole and some others have convinced the University that the whole issue can't come before the Ad-ministrative Council while there's any question about Cud-lipp's death. So, if there's anything I can do to help you . . ."

"You're certain in your own mind then that no one connected with the University College could have given him the aspirin?"

"Yes. That sort of thing just doesn't occur to academic people, Mr. Amhearst."

"You'd be surprised what occurs to academic people these days, Dean Frogmore. Let me tell you something about the D.A.'s Office that has changed since your now historical events last spring. It used to be if a college kid got into trouble, if anyone connected with the academic world got into trouble, the lawyer would come to the D.A.'s Office and say 'Look, he's a college kid, you don't want to press charges.' And we didn't press charges. If you were connected with a university or college it was assumed you were probably straight; certainly you got the benefit of the doubt and then some. Now? All the D.A.'s Office has to hear is it's a college kid, and they're pressing charges so fast the lawyer can't even follow the handwriting. As troublemakers, the members of the academic world have lost their amateur standing. The question here is: did you know about Cudlipp's allergy to aspirin?"

"I did know, though I'd forgotten I knew. Bill McQuire reminded me. A while back he said something about Cudlipp being so tensed up he was living on those British pills of his. I thought Bill was referring to birth-control pills, actually, which is what the word 'pill' seems to mean these days, and I said I didn't get it. Then Bill told me about Cudlipp's headaches and how he couldn't take ordinary aspirin. But believe it or not, Mr. Amhearst, the news just didn't sink in; it wasn't of interest."

"Do you think the students knew of it?"

"I can't imagine how. But my experience with students like Peabody is that they know everything there is to know, and a lot that hasn't been thought up yet. I wonder if Miss Philips was able . . ."

"Dean Frogmore, what did you feel about Cudlipp personally? I mean, did you have the sense he was not a bad guy underneath, did you think he would give in in the end, had you become fond of him for all his prejudice and churlishness, or did you dislike him rather intensely? I'm not looking for a motive, sir. The motive is screaming itself all over the place. I'd just like a sense of the sort of feelings Cudlipp aroused in someone outside the English Department."

"I hated him, and so did all of those in the inner circle of old-timers here. There's no sense side-stepping that. I think the man was demented, if you want to know the truth, and so beside himself with vengeance and rage that he was perfectly capable of not knowing aspirin from peppermint Life Savers. I realize there is a lot of pressure from the College alumni, and I know the University is hard-up for funds right now—student disruption hardly stimulates giving—and that our alumni don't fork it over the way the College alumni do, but none of that explains his animus. I don't mind admitting that if I could have got Cudlipp an unrefusable offer from somewhere a thousand miles away, I would have grabbed at the chance; but that's a long way from murder."

"From all I've heard, part of Cudlipp's dementia was his devotion to the College. Apparently neither he nor Clemance would ever consider going anywhere else. And of course, Dean Frogmore," Reed said, rising, "whoever gave Cudlipp the aspirin wasn't necessarily planning murder; aspirin allergies are dangerous, but rarely fatal." Reed had planned to exit on that line, but there came a knock at the door. Miss Philips stuck her head in. "John Peabody is here, Dean Frogmore."

Frogmore introduced them: "John, this is Mr. Amhearst."

"Hi," John Peabody said. "How about some lunch?" Clearly, informality was going to be Mr. Peabody's keynote.

"Fine," Reed said. "Thank you, Dean Frogmore. I may be back with more questions, if you'll allow me, but I can't think of any more at the moment."

"Any time, any time," Frogmore said. "Glad to have you aboard."

"You must really be Some-Body," Peabody said as they walked out, making it two words. "You the D.A. or just his brother?"

"Has something noteworthy occurred?"

"Frogmore never called you by your first name. Man, he must really be impressed."

"I never told him my first name."

"He picks up first names the way radar picks up moving objects. Regular bar and grill O.K. by you? We might even have a beer."

"Suits me," Reed said. He found himself amused by John Peabody, who looked not only as though he had slept in his clothes, but as though he had spent his whole honeymoon in them. Why wear a tie when it is not tied, a shirt when it is not buttoned, Reed wondered? Still, his tie is not psychedelic and he does not wear beads; there is always much to be thankful for.

The 'regular bar and grill' turned out to be a largish restaurant with beer on draught, and Reed settled comfortably into a booth with John Peabody, who fetched them each a stein. "Here's to it," Peabody said. "I didn't bump Cudlipp off, but, brother, I sure would have, given the chance. Man, we used to have fantasies—me and the other guys at U.C. Maybe we'd kidnap his kids and say, 'O.K., mac, you get them back when you lay off old U.C.' We dreamed about holding him prisoner in a cellar and beating him with wet ropes until he begged for mercy, and then we planned to say: 'After you call the Acting President, mac, and make it O.K. about old U.C.' So help me, if I'd known of this aspirin dodge, I'd have forced them down his stinking throat myself. He actually pushed me out of his office. I know he's old enough to be my father, which would have made it one great big pleasure to lay him out flat, but he closed the door, and the other guys held onto me." Peabody concluded with a few up-to-date epithets. Odd, Reed thought: When we were young we mouthed niceties and thought nastily. Mr. Peabody sounds like a horror and it's perfectly obvious he's nice as pie underneath. At least, so I assume.

"I thought two of the students with you were women?"

"Sure. And Randy Selkirk. All good guys."

"I see. What happened exactly?"

"You want a sandwich? I'll be glad to get us each one, if you've got what it takes. I'm stony."

Solemnly Reed handed over some money. "Ham and cheese on rye for me," he said.

Peabody returned in short order—clearly he was known here and got immediate service—with two sandwiches and two more steins of beer and a pack of cigarettes. "You need cigarettes?" he asked Reed.

"I gather," Reed said, "that you are fresh out."

"Man, you learn fast," Peabody said. "We like your bird."

"I'm lost again," Reed said. "I thought it was ham and cheese."

"Professor Fansler, man. She's your bird. Fun and games in the Graduate English Office, when Cudlipp took the wrong pills. She's real sexy on the Victorian novel."

"Sexy?"

"Good, man, good."

"Yes," Reed said. "Thank you. Now—about your meeting with Cudlipp. Could you give it to me slowly and in something approximating standard English?"

"There's nothing to give. We went there, the four of us, armed with our stories. We're used to giving them—we did that bit for your bi—for Professor Fansler. The point is to give someone an idea of how great U.C. is. What it's meant to us. We're all different types, but all kind of impressive, if you follow me. But I hadn't even finished my piece—I sort of M.C. the show—when Cudlipp lost his cool; man, he flipped. I found out why after: I'd said something about U.C. not just being a place to take some courses and wile away the time—I always say that—and of course he'd been bounced from *The* College a hundred years ago, when he was a lad, and had taken courses at U.C., then called extension, to wile away the time till he could get back in with the upperclass lads.''

"Did anyone else say anything?"

"Didn't have a chance. He went for me. The others had to help me—boy, I was powed. But that Barbara Campbell is a cool chick. After they all got me out, and before Cudlipp could slam the door, she turned to him— of course her clothes are by Dior out of Bergdorf—and said, 'Professor Cudlipp, a man of your standing should have better control of himself.' Just like that. He slammed the door so hard I thought its hinges would spring off. And that's all there is to that story.''

"Not much help, I'm afraid," Reed said. "You optimistic about the Administrative Council's actions?"

"Well, we got to clear up this mess. What about the elevators, man, carrying on like that. Beer tastes better in a stein, don't you think, and certainly better on draught. Want another?"

"No, thanks. What about the elevators?"

"What about them?"

"Didn't you say . . ."

"Man, you better take it easy. You're pushing too hard."

"Right." Reed pocketed his change. "It was a pleasure, Mr. Peabody."

"Likewise. Take it . . ."

"I know," Reed said. "I plan to."

Reed had an appointment downtown; one cannot, after all, spend one's entire day vamping and drinking beer with undergraduates, but he dropped into Castleman's office, just on the chance. Castleman was, Reed learned, at lunch at the Faculty Club. Reed said thanks and strolled toward the Faculty Club, not quite clear in his mind what he wanted to ask Castleman, but figuring he better have a look at the Club anyway, since that seemed to be where everybody spent all their time laying plans, nefarious or other. Entering the Club, he met Castleman coming out.

"Ah," Castleman said, stepping aside with Reed. "Any progress?"

"Tell me," Reed said, "is there somebody in the administration with whom I could discuss elevators?"

"Will I do? Or do you want the maintenance department?"

"I'm not sure what I want. I take it my question does not surprise you."

"Not unbearably. Shall we sit down a minute? Have you had lunch?"

Reed nodded. "Let me just say 'elevators' and you tell me what comes into your mind."

"The Acting President mentioned it to me this morning, as it happens. I never thought of there being a connection with the Cudlipp business—but of course he was caught in an elevator, wasn't he?"

"Fatally, as it turned out. Or probably so."

"I see. This has got to be strictly confidential, Mr. Amhearst. Not part of any report or officially noticed at all."

"I have seldom found any use for information that isn't off the record," Reed said, "but if an actionable crime has been committed, I can't blink it away."

"No, naturally not. I was referring to the general University problem. But I know, who better, that you can't ask someone to do a job and then bury him in *caveats*. The trouble with discretion in a university, I've been learning, is that if a man is discreet, it turns out his friends are the only ones in the dark. Everyone else, of course, has

been consulting like mad. The line between full consulta-
tion and decent discretion is finer than the razor's edge.
Well, elevators. The elevators in the University have
always been a blasted nuisance, an irritating joke. They
are much overused, and by a community of youngsters
whose gentleness with feedback devices is not noticeable.
Still, it was never a serious problem. What usually happens is that an elevator which you have ridden for what
seems like millennia in order to reach the top floor
would decide one floor from the top that it was going no
higher, and deposit you back on the ground floor minus
two. Like that game my kids keep playing where you
land on the wrong square and return to go. Annoying,
but all in a day's work. Quite often the elevators going
down would simply refuse to stop at all, but we always
suspected they were secretly geared that way as a hint that
we ought to walk down."

"I lived once in a *pension* in Paris," Reed said, "where
you were only allowed to take the elevator up. I found it
extremely annoying at times, particularly if one were
descending with heavy packages."

"It is annoying. But that was about the size of it until
this fall. Then, elevators began stopping between floors,
sometimes in one building and sometimes in another.
There was a great rash of that, and then the elevators took
to stopping only during special hours, days or evenings
when there was a meeting in a building, or all the deans
were on their way to see the President, or, for example,
when the whole senior classics faculty was in the elevator.
Occasionally an hysterical student would get stuck and
have to be treated for shock. Only very recently did we
officially begin to wonder if it was actually part of some
subversive plan."

"To what end?"

"Disruption. Confusion. One more inducement to lose
confidence and believe in the general ineptness of uni-

versities. It's a clever trick, really, better in its way than class disruption, because no one's caught at it, no one organizes against it, and its effects are more subtle and therefore longer lasting."

"You mean objectless hostility builds up?"

"Exactly. Anger, or hostility if you prefer the term, is one of those forces modern society hasn't devised any really good way of dealing with. Kicking an elevator you're locked into, or an elevator door which shows no sign of opening, is humiliating and unsatisfactory—so one takes it out instead on the next student or colleague one meets. Yet stopping elevators isn't really a major crime. Whoever does it probably isn't even trespassing, according to the letter of the law, and they aren't really causing any damage that can be laid directly to them. Always supposing we knew who 'they' are."

"But how are the elevators stopped, do you know? It sounds a bit dangerous."

"That's what had puzzled us for so long. This whole business seemed to require a high degree of technical knowledge and timing. Then one day we nearly caught one of the culprits, or at least, Cartier thinks he nearly caught him. Cartier had dashed to the basement of the building once when he heard an elevator stop, just in time to see someone sneaking out. Cartier, who has more nerve than sense if you want to know, almost grabbed the guy, but not quite. Anyway, when he looked at the place where the miscreant had been standing he discovered the power box."

"So they simply turned off the juice?"

"As simple as that. We couldn't lock the damn thing; one has to be able to get at it in case of emergencies. The campus guards tried keeping an eye on the elevators, but, needless to say, they couldn't be everywhere at once. No doubt someone was waiting to tamper with the elevator in Baldwin the night Cudlipp died, knowing there was

136

something going on up there. Simple enough, when you figure it out."

"Is this the sort of thing these radical groups go in for?"

"No, it isn't. That's the most surprising aspect of the whole thing. They want publicity, some big, showy gesture which embarrasses the greatest number of people in the most flamboyant possible way, and puts the authorities immediately on the spot."

"The word is confrontation, isn't it?"

"Exactly. Whereas confrontation is what one doesn't have here. Just a rather diabolic scheme by someone who's more interested in annoying the University than confronting it; someone with a twisted sense of humor; if you want my guess, it'll turn out to be someone who got bounced out of here and is still simmering. The sort of people who used to sue the University for failing to fulfill its contract after they had flunked out, in the good old quiet days. But it's anyone's guess."

"Well," Reed said, rising, "it's not a pretty mess, but I don't suppose it's got anything to do with the present investigations."

"Let me know if I can be of help in any other way. There's no question that time . . . Hi, Bill. I'd like you to meet Reed Amhearst from the D.A.'s Office; he's looking into Cudlipp's death. Bill McQuire."

"If you're walking to the subway, Mr. Amhearst, I'll go with you and see if I can be of any help. My office is in that direction. You interest me."

"Do I? Why?"

"Lots of reasons. Let's say I think it's going to be uphill work, finding out who slipped those aspirin into Cudlipp's pocket supply. Let's say, what I happen to believe, that the University killed him."

"Now that's an interesting idea. Why?"

"Because he was doing his best to kill the University. Oh, he thought he was saving it, of course. But he was pushing the College out of all proportion. I think he would have been willing to see the rest of the University go if he could have used the resources for The College. Even if you could find out how the aspirin got into Mrs. Murphy's chowder, would it matter?"

"It seems it will matter to the University College quite a lot. The Administrative Council won't move if this matter isn't cleared up."

Bill McQuire whistled. "That sounds like the work of our friend O'Toole. Well, it's the last gasp. Do you know everyone Cudlipp saw? Someone must have done some hanky-panky with those pills of his."

"I've got a pretty good line on most of them now. What do you think of Cartier?"

"He's in the English Department; hated Cudlipp's guts, but that hardly makes him even noticeable in that crowd. I'm an economist myself."

"Someone suggested, in passing, that Cartier was perhaps somewhat hot-headed."

"He is. He doesn't talk much, but he's always popping around and turning up in odd places. During the police bust last spring, he was hit on the head by a policeman and carried off in a paddy wagon and damn near charged before anyone identified him, and all because he got into an argument with a student about the indecency of calling any human beings, even policemen, pigs. When he got out the students said surely he'd changed his mind, but he said no, policemen were unnecessarily brutal, probably sadistic, and certainly ill-advised, but they weren't pigs."

"Might he have been impulsive enough to pull the aspirin trick?"

"I can't see it. He and I saw Cudlipp together the day he died."

"I know."

"Were you working up to asking me about it? Because I've got to make a class in a minute." Reed nodded. "We tried to urge Cudlipp to soft-peddle it a bit, but he wasn't having any. Cartier said . . ."

"Yes?"

"He said, 'You're asking for trouble, Cudlipp; violence and trouble.' But I'm sure he was just speaking generally."

"What did you say to Cudlipp?"

"I told him if he kept on the way he was going, someone would break his goddam neck for him. Well, let me know if I can help."

Reed took the subway downtown and was so engrossed in the problem that he forgot to get off at Franklin Street.

Mr. Higgenbothom turned up promptly at four.

"And how," Kate asked, "are the computers?"

"You must let me show you through the computer center one of these days."

"I should like that," Kate said. "If only I had a problem a computer could solve this very moment. But I gather computers can give you answers only if you give them all the relevant information and ask all the right questions. Alas, I haven't either."

Mr. Higgenbothom sat down and looked politely expectant.

"As you have no doubt heard," Kate rather ponderously began, "Professor Cudlipp died at a party given in my honor the other evening." Mr. Higgenbothom nodded. "His death was, of course, the result of several unfortunate accidents, but the University would like, if possible, to establish some of the facts surrounding the case. Which means, in English that cats and dogs can understand, that I want a worm's-eye view of the College English Department—and what is nearer a worm than a teaching assistant?"

Mr. Higgenbothom grinned.

"And," Kate went on, "if you say a word about discretion, I will throw something at you. I am willing to let you use a computer on Max Beerbohm, who couldn't even stand the simpler inventions of the twentieth century, so you've got to be willing to let me have your impressions— at least, I hope you'll be willing."

"I could quote Max Beerbohm in connection with Professor Cudlipp," Mr. Higgenbothom said. "If two people disagree about a third, the one who likes him is right, always."

"I'm to gather that you liked Cudlipp?"

"Yes, very much. He was very nice to me indeed. He let me experiment with my freshman English group—I spent the whole year on linguistics and stylistics and the students actually liked it—but it took some believing in me on his part. And then, he was very devoted to the College, and so am I. He believed it could really be an exciting educational place, because we were all ready to experiment, and Robert O'Toole was going to be Dean and do the first exciting things to be brought off in education in the last forty years. I know Cudlipp didn't think highly of the University College, and I understand that you believe in it, but he knew perfectly well that there had to be only one undergraduate school here, and that first-rate. I agreed with him, and still do. I think Cudlipp had courage and he worked for what he believed in. I admire that. So many men just let things slide."

Kate leaned back in her chair and laughed. "Sorry," she said to Mr. Higgenbothom when she had recovered herself. "I'm laughing at my getting so cocksure as to forget there are two sides to every question, and I damn well ought to remember that. Would you be willing to tell me who's likely to be new head of the College English Department?"

"At the moment it seems to be a standoff. I hear there's been some heated discussion."

"Between whom, mainly?"

"You're remembering, Professor Fansler, that this is a worm's-eye view?"

"By all means. I would apologize for asking these forthright questions when you can scarcely avoid answering them, Mr. Higgenbothom, if there were the smallest point in apologizing for what one has every intention of doing."

"The rumor is that Clemance wants us to think about it a bit, sort of struggle on for a few months and not put a Cudlipp man right in. He says he's willing to take on some of the work for the rest of the term, and no one's exactly prepared to argue with that. I'm sorry there are more ill feelings; we ought to be healing up the wounds. We're getting together a memorial volume to Cudlipp, by the way. I hope you'll feel better about him by the time it comes out, which, given the schedules of scholars and university presses, should be in about three years."

"I'm certain to feel better about him long before then. Thank you for coming, and good luck with Max's sentences."

In fact, it was one of Max's sentences Kate quoted to Reed when he asked her how her day had gone. " 'To give an accurate and exhaustive account of that period would need a far less brilliant pen than mine,' " she wearily said.

"Likewise," said Reed. It was uncertain what a computer would have made of that.

CHAPTER NINE

Our race would not have gotten far,
Had we not learned to bluff it out
And look more certain than we are
Of what our motion is about.

The week that followed was marked for Kate not primarily by attempts to solve the puzzle of the elevators and the aspirin, but by the presence together of Reed and herself on the campus. She was startled to discover that she had always held the University and Reed quite separate in her mind, as though her place of work existed, as far as Reed was concerned, as the source of news and problems and experiences which she might bring home and lay as tribute at his feet.

But now he had joined her in the problems and experience and news, and she found she enjoyed enormously walking with him on the campus, bidding him at its center a formal farewell which seemed to include their love more easily than any public embrace could ever have done. Reed, for his part, admitted the fascination of the campus and his eagerness to leave it as having equal force with him. Certainly he did not want to leave it until he could provide it with the knowledge it required for peace. Disruptions of communities, like illnesses, are not cured by being named; but if one names them, one isolates them from their allies: unreasoning fear, anxiety, and trepidation. The magic of doctors, for all their research, Reed pointed out to Kate, is still their power to name. He had the power now; he wanted to use it and be gone.

In the past week Kate had had probing conversations with such involved students and faculty as she met and, since the troubles of spring, one seemed constantly to meet people and to stop and talk. From resembling a club where only the oldest members recognized and spoke to one another, the University had come to seem like a small town where everyone knew and greeted one another, and usually had news, gossip, or rumors to exchange. As always, Kate thought, it was danger and shared experiences which made the modern world like a village—not. television, as that dreary medium-message man had said. She had talked to many and learned a good deal, but none of it seemed to move them very far forward.

Frogmore reported that he had talked with almost all the members of the Administrative Council, and there was no question that University College had an overwhelming number of votes with which to carry their motion *if* they could ever get it before the Council. A number of members on the Council came from schools not immediately connected with the Undergraduate or Graduate Faculties of Arts and Sciences, and they clearly saw no reason why one branch of the University should be able to eliminate another—not without more cogent reasons than were being mentioned. Frogmore, as he told Kate, only hoped it would be that simple.

McQuire, who sought Kate out to tell her how superior he thought Reed, said that he now believed Cudlipp had committed suicide as the best way to kill the University College. "Call it a kind of hari-kari," he had said. " 'I'll go down and take the enemy ship with me.' " In that case, Kate had pointed out, it would have made more sense to accuse his putative murderer before collapsing instead of merely yelling "aspirin" in that unhelpful way. McQuire only shrugged. "There is no question," he said, "that the whole plan went awry. We shall probably never know. He has succeeded all the same, and I'm powerfully gloomy. Let's get a drink."

But Kate had gone on to talk to Cartier, who was beginning to intrigue her a good deal. He was the most restless man Kate had ever seen, almost as though he suffered from some muscular ailment which caused him to begin twitching if he stood or sat in one place too long. He would greet one pleasantly enough, with some provocative remark ("I'm on my way to interfere with a few elevators, how are you?" was a fair example) but after extracting a certain amount of information and imparting as little as he decently could he would twitch away as though some unseen string attached to him had been jerked offstage. A good deal of his restlessness, Kate surmised, came from his hunger for information and his utter inability to impart any. Since most people would rather talk than listen, Cartier's method worked up to a point. He would listen, nodding furiously, and then, when questioned in turn, would depart in a stammered explanation of pressing engagements. But after a time Kate, and no doubt others, began to realize that the exchange of information was not mutual, that Cartier could not bring himself to trust anyone else's discretion. Kate faced him with this one day, and he accepted it, in his usual curt style, nodding his head and thrusting out his arms in his puppet fashion. "What elevators, for example, are you going to interfere with?" "Oh, just a joke, just a joke," he replied, retreating exactly, it seemed to Kate, like some actress playing Tinkerbell whose apparatus is not working properly.

On the day when she had talked to McQuire she had gone to look for Cartier in the lounge of the Faculty Club. It was the best place to pick up information, and Cartier could never avoid it for long. She had, indeed, found Cartier and, with great difficulty, induced him to sit down with her on a couch. He offered every possible excuse, from imminent disasters to rising ill health, but Kate was firm: "I'll only keep you a minute. Please sit down. I'm not feeling at all well." This, while untrue, made Cartier's refusal impossible. He perched on the couch, his weight on his toes and his knees drawn up, for all the world, Kate had thought, like a Victorian maiden lady anticipating an indecent proposal. Yet, Kate had thought, he is the only man I know who can resemble Little Miss Muffet without looking in the least effeminate.

She had reported McQuire's theory to him. "Interesting," was his comment, "but I don't believe it. The aspirin were merely the result of an unfortunate accident, pharmaceutical more likely than not; no one seems to have thought of that. The important question is the elevators." Cartier always stopped talking as abruptly as he began, one of his more appealing characteristics these long-winded days.

"Have any elevators been stopping lately that you know of?" Kate had asked. "And," she had added ominously, "if you try to leave I shall sit in your lap until you answer me."

"Wonderful," Cartier had surprisingly said, pushing himself back on the couch to make more lap available.

"I'm sorry," Kate had said. "The ultimate sin: pigeon-holing people, thinking you always know what they will say." Cartier took the apology as dismissal, but then paused as Kate allowed her unanswered question about the elevators to echo between them.

"There's a meeting of the Chemistry Department late this afternoon," he had said, departing. Kate had remained on the couch, treasuring this piece of information. She could not imagine what possible use it could be, but it was the only fact which Cartier had ever imparted to her. It was unfortunate that she had not taken it more to heart, or at least reported it immediately to Reed, because when she ran into Professor Fielding of Chemistry several days later, he mentioned that the whole Graduate Chemistry Faculty had been stuck in the science building elevator for forty-five minutes on the day of their meeting.

Reed in the past week had interviewed maintenance men, guards, deans, secretaries, and receptionists until he was weary of endless opinions on the student generation, dire predictions about the future, and completely useless information. He told Kate as they emerged from the subway in time for her afternoon seminar that he hoped today would yield something, but he doubted it.

In this he was wrong.

To begin with, they ran into Castleman. He stopped to talk to them, resting his briefcase on the ground. "I have seen more progress," he said, "made by an inchworm on frictionless terrain. Oh, not your fault, not mine, not anybody's. Cartier thinks he'll catch someone at the elevators, but it will be the same story over again. Whoever is doing this isn't going to walk into any trap. If someone's there, they go away; if someone comes in on them, they run faster."

"Is there a meeting of some sort today?"

"Yes. Political Science."

"Why haven't you tried to keep these meetings secret?" Kate asked.

"We thought of it—and then we thought a bit more. First of all, it's impossible; if you have a meeting of eight people, there are at least double that number or more in the world who have to know it; we aren't running a secret organization, God forbid. Besides, our only chance is either to get the offenders to stop out of sheer boredom, or to catch them. It isn't as though there were any real danger; people terrified of being caught in elevators walk—they always have at this place anyway. Let's face it, the elevators, even in the best of times, were problematical."

"What time is the meeting?" Reed asked.

"Four. It could go on till six. And chances are nothing will happen." He wearily picked up his briefcase and left them.

Kate and Reed continued across the campus, feeling defeated and eager to act if only some possible action presented itself. Reed was just leaving Kate at the entrance to Baldwin when Clemance came along.

"You two," he announced, "the first really pleasant sight in days." He smiled his characteristic, sideways smile and stopped a moment with his oddly courteous air, implying that if they had anything to say he was delighted to hear it, but that he was bereft of the power of speech.

"I must be getting very old indeed," he finally murmured. "I actually find myself dreaming of the old days here, when we attended chapel in our gowns with fair regularity. I suppose what I'm trying to say is that this used to be a world of gentlemen, and I wish it still were. Nostalgia is a dangerous disease."

"You're just gloomy about this Cudlipp business, and no wonder," Kate said, really worried about him. "What's dangerous about nostalgia is that it's phony. It's a day-dream in reverse. Like thinking we loved the books of our youth, when all we love is the thought of ourselves young, reading them."

"You're right. I resent so much being old, and being thought stuffy, that out of a kind of childish petulance I talk as though I were considerably older than I am. I don't mind telling you there are moments when, quite apart from wanting Cudlipp back again, I wish that someone had handed me a poison, instead of him."

"You must be pleased about O'Toole becoming Dean of the College."

"I guess I must. My daughter's going to have a baby."

"One's daughter's having a baby must, in a certain way, be the most shocking thing that can happen to a man," Reed said. "I've seen it often."

"You're probably right," Clemance said. "Anyway, it's getting to be winter, and that's always dreary. Let's hope that this will be a better spring—that the grass will not be trampled to dry earth, or the tulips crushed and broken." He raised his hat and left them.

"So he noticed exactly what I did—the death of the grass and flowers. The war-torn countryside is always desolate; grass only grows later, among the crosses."

"For God's sake, Kate, I'm glad you at least waited till he was gone to make that heartening observation."

"I can't see making him greet a grandchild as the mark of doom as exactly designed to cheer him up."

"It at least gives him a natural cause for feeling glum, instead of despair about the University. Where does the Political Science Department keep itself?"

"In Treadwell Hall—over there."

"I'm going to reconnoiter. Kate . . ."

"Yes?" Kate said when he did not seem to be continuing.

"Oh, nothing. I'll see you later."

"Yes. I must give some thought to my seminar. We all of us spend so much time at committee meetings that we forget what we're really here for." She waved at Reed as she walked away.

Reed waited, he scarcely knew for what, in the basement of Treadwell Hall. It was dimly lit and unfinished. Reconnoitering, he had discovered the door leading to the tunnels connecting the buildings. They had been used for years, Kate told him, by professors who did not want to emerge into the cold in winter, the rain in spring, or student greetings at any time. Another door apparently hid some machinery which made a good deal of noise but seemed otherwise of no interest. The box with the switches for the elevator was, as might have been expected, in the darkest corner. Reed looked at his watch.

He went back upstairs and out onto the campus and walked about, thinking.

When he returned it was to contemplate the extremely wide pipes that ran along the basement about a foot from the ceiling. He jumped for one, but found he could not reach high enough to pull himself upward. He tried a running jump, but the basement did not provide adequate leaping room. Finally, he opened the door leading to the tunnel and pulled himself up on it until one of his feet rested on the knob. As he climbed he had to keep pushing the door, whose nature was to close itself, open with his other foot. At last he worked himself into a position to swing from the door onto one of the broad pipes. The door, relieved of his weight, closed. He was able to lie across the broad pipe on his stomach, resting his head on his hands. He was not invisible to anyone who looked up, but people do not normally look up in empty basements. Should he be discovered, Reed thought, he would merely go about the business of climbing down and make as dignified an exit as was possible under the circumstances. But he hoped to remain unnoticed long enough to see who came, and why.

His position was not uncomfortable. It interested him to realize that for all the physical vigor of the storybook detective, this was the only time he had had the crease in his trousers endangered by anything more extraordinary than the heat of a courtroom. After a time, he began almost to doze.

But not quite. As the door from the stairway opened, he came fully awake. A man entered silently and hurried noiselessly across the basement to the door behind which was housed the machinery. He opened the door with a key and, reaching inside, extracted first a wooden doorstop with which he braced open the door, and then a long, hollow tube with which he moved to the center of the room. Raising the tube above his head, he proceeded to slip it over the light bulb and turn it until the light went out. Fortunately the man, who was Cartier, had his back to Reed while he worked. Having plunged the basement into darkness, Cartier, carrying his tube, retreated into the machinery room and closed the door behind him. All was dark and silent.

Not long after, the door from the stairway opened again, and another man entered—Reed could not, in the darkness, tell who it was. The new arrival walked over to the corner near where the power box for the elevator was and crouched down, resting, Reed supposed, on his heels. Again there was silence. For a great period of time, it seemed, they waited. Periodically, Reed could hear the elevator motor start up and then stop. He longed to switch his position on the pipe, but dared not. From time to time he felt rather than heard the man in the corner shift his weight.

Up in Mabel's room, Reed thought, and we shall all be here until morning. And at the thought of explaining to Kate how he had happened to spend a whole night on a pipe in the basement of Treadwell Hall, Reed began to feel himself hideously on the verge of the giggles, about the only calamity, he thought, which never befell Sam Spade or Philip Marlowe.

How long it was until the door from the stairway opened was a question which might well have inspired agonized deliberations about the relativity of time. When the door did open, however, whoever entered was clearly bewildered to find himself in darkness. He listened—as Reed, holding his breath, listened, as the other two, he was certain, listened; but there was no sound. Running his hands along the wall to find his way, the last arrival moved around until he was in front of the elevator. Reed saw him take out a tiny pocket flashlight and consult his wristwatch. Before long, the elevator machinery could be heard running: the elevator had been called, one supposed, to a

top floor. There was a pause as the light which indicates
when the elevator is in motion went out; then it lit again.
The listeners could hear the elevator descending. The
newcomer moved toward the box containing the elevator
power switch and the silence broke into clamoring noise.
The door to the machine room was flung open, several
men seemed to be grabbing one another, there was a
scuffle toward the doors, Reed heard a man's voice whisper: "For God's sake get out of here," and then there was
the sound of a pressurized can being sprayed. "You goddam idiot," the same voice whispered. By this time Reed
had dropped down from the pipe and was guarding the
door to the stairway. A man rushed against him and they
were both propelled into the lighted stairway hall. The
man with Reed was Hankster, and he was covered with
bright, luminous paint. As they stared at each other,
speechless, they were joined by Cartier who simply
announced "Ha!" in pleased tones, and refused to utter
another syllable. The fourth man there, whoever he was,
had vanished.

It took several hours to straighten the whole thing out, if
"to straighten out," as Reed later said to Kate, was possibly the correct verb.

Cartier was mightily pleased with the success of his "spy
kit." He had apparently begun his James Bond operations
with a camera equipped with extremely fast film or, in
the event of almost total darkness, a strobe light. This, he
readily admitted, had been a dismal failure. Either he
was not quick enough in handling the equipment, or the
camera was not focused on anything very enlightening.
Cartier had already, he said, come close enough to touch
at least two of the elevator interferers, but even if he
pursued them into a lighted area, they mingled with
groups of students too quickly for him to feel certain of
identifying them. Hence the pressurized paint can: it cov-

ered its victim with paint so that he could be readily recognized; melting away into a crowd would not be possible.

The only problem in this case was, as Hankster pointed out to Cartier in agonized whispers, the wrong man had been sprayed, the wrong man's expensive clothes had been ruined, and they had all made idiots of themselves.

"Then what *were* you doing there?" Cartier had not unnaturally asked.

"Trying to prevent a misguided youngster from getting himself into serious trouble for the wrong cause," Hankster said.

"One of your radical students, no doubt," Cartier said.

"Perhaps, as you say, a radical student, though hardly mine. The idea of disrupting the University by elevator hanky-panky did not originate with me, or him, or any radical in the ordinary sense of the word."

"With whom, then, did it originate?" Reed asked.

"Cudlipp, of course," Hankster said. "Didn't you guess?"

They both stared at him for a moment. "And," Reed asked, before Cartier could make some remark as rude as it was concise, "would you be willing to arrange for us to meet one of the students involved in this at Cudlipp's instigation?"

"No," Hankster said. "I'll do my best to stop this business, if I have enough influence to accomplish it, enough persuasive powers, and am not poisoned by all this paint, but I won't give you a single name. Sorry about that."

He marched out, probably the first man, as Kate later observed, to desert a conversation with Cartier before Cartier did.

"But," Kate asked Reed that night, "can Hankster's accusation possibly be true?"

CHAPTER
TEN

A truth at which one should arrive,
Forbids immediate utterance,
And tongues to speak it must contrive
To tell two different lies at once.

The following morning's mail brought an invitation to a poetry reading from the Graduate Students' English Society. The GSES, clearly proud of itself, announced its poet with a flourish and a photograph: W. H. Auden. Kate looked with pleasure at the picture of the white, marvelously rumpled face. Of Icelandic descent, Auden possessed, in the words of Christopher Isherwood, "hair like bleached straw and thick, coarse-looking, curiously white flesh, as though every drop of blood had been pumped out of his body." The lines in Auden's face, originally formed, Isherwood said, by "the misleadingly ferocious frown common to people of very short sight," had, over the years, deepened and softened: the expression, Kate thought, looking at the photograph, was less ferocious than experienced, life-tossed. She looked forward to the poetry reading. I wonder, she thought, if Clemance will be going. It seems, somehow, suitable that he and I and Auden should be in the same room together in these strange days. But of course he knows Auden and will probably want to see him first.

It would all have to be arranged soon. Auden's reading was not far off and must have been arranged hurriedly, but the new GSES was doing well. The previous organization of Graduate English students had, in fact, belonged to the students only nominally; the faculty had used it to try out members from other institutions whom it might later choose to woo. Since the revolution, the GSES had been wrested from faculty hands and devoted to readings and discussion which the students thought interesting: everyone considered the arrangement a wonderful improvement as God knows it is, Kate thought, marking the date down on her calendar.

She was interrupted in this observation by the ringing of the telephone. Clemance, as though in answer to her thought, asked if she were going to the reading and if she would accompany him. Auden, Clemance said, would not be dining at the University but would arrive just for the reading. Somewhat astonished, Kate agreed to meet Clemance outside the auditorium. "I had just opened the invitation myself," she said, "and was thinking that you must be planning to go."

"Oh, yes," Clemance said. "I have always, of course, admired his poetry, but it is truly eerie how near he is to the bone these days. Do you know the lines:

> *What have you done to them?*
> *Nothing? Nothing is not an answer:*
> *You will come to believe—how can you help it?—*
> *That you did, you did do something;*
> *You will find yourself wishing you could make them*
> *laugh;*
> *You will long for their friendship.*

He is so right in those lines," Clemance went on, "about how one feels, even toward those students who have most cavalierly and with least thought destroyed the confidence and cordiality it took years to establish. And so right, of course, about guilt. We who in the turmoil of today can continue to believe that we did nothing—we are the generation, are we not, who is finished? Will you bring Reed Amhearst?"

"To the reading? Certainly, if he wants to come; he hears so much Auden these days he's quoting it himself. But I suspect there will be an awful mob."

"I think I can reserve three seats," Clemance said. "My influence, though waning, extends that far. A quarter of eight then, Friday evening?"

When he had rung off Kate pondered a bit about the fancy Clemance had taken to Reed, who appeared oddly skittish in the presence of the famous professor. Certainly that remark about the horrors of daughters having babies had been the absolutely most uncharacteristic remark she had ever heard Reed make. Well, it was probably one of the happier effects of the turmoil that people no longer sorted themselves out so neatly. Reed, indeed, had become a more rigorous attender of the University than she. He was there now, hanging from pipes no doubt and contemplating elevators.

Reed, at that moment, was thinking of elevators, though not hanging from pipes. He was in fact smack in the middle of the campus contemplating Hankster's suggestion about Cudlipp. A red herring? The determining factor was, of course, when precisely . . . Reed turned his steps toward the Administration Building.

"To see President Matthewson now?" The secretary was clearly unhappy, and Reed could well guess why. The Acting President, compensating for the almost total inaccessibility of his predecessor, had made a point of being readily available to all comers. But of course, in his position, this was a difficult principle to implement: one could scarcely allow oneself to be broken in on by every petulant complainer at every hour of the day. So Matthewson's much-tried secretary had learned to parry requests. "But," she plaintively said, "he's in an important conference."

"Tell me, Miss Franklin," Reed said, reading her name from the sign on her desk, "do you remember when you were called by two faculty members who were stuck in an elevator?"

"I certainly do," Miss Franklin said with emphasis. "A *most* disturbing conversation."

"Did you subsequently report it to President Matthewson?"

"I told him about it that very afternoon. He chuckled, in fact. But of course when more and more faculty members started getting stuck in elevators, and senior faculty for the most part. . . ."

"His chuckles became noticeably less robust, as I can well imagine. Tell me, Miss Franklin, and please be sure of your answer: was that occasion when Professors Everglade and Fansler called you from the elevator the first time senior faculty, shall we say as a group, were stuck in an elevator between floors?"

"Oh, yes, I can be quite certain about that. In fact, President Matthewson mentioned it again to me only the other day."

"I see. Miss Franklin, I'm sure you will be immeasurably relieved to know that I no longer have any need to see President Matthewson. His conference may continue undisturbed, at least by me."

"I'm exceedingly glad to be of help," Miss Franklin faintly said. She did not pretend to understand the conversation she had just taken part in, but if a crisis, in these days of continuing crises, had been averted by the exchange of inconclusive remarks, she was not about to complain.

Feeling considerably more buoyant than he had in days, Reed set off for the bar and grill where he had lunched with Peabody. The man, Reed thought, who speaks in two languages, one in a university and one in a bar and grill. He called Kate my bird, said she was sexy about the Victorian novel, told me nothing, made me pay for the lunch, and yet left me with the feeling that I had profited by the whole occasion. Which I had.

Sure enough, Mr. Peabody was in his accustomed booth, drinking beer and holding forth.

"May I ask you a question privately?" Reed asked. Peabody stepped aside with Reed.

"I sometimes take the Fifth, but probably not with you," he said.

"Do you remember," Reed asked, "the day you and three of your fellow University College students, who are, I understand, a sort of traveling P.R. arrangement for your Alma Mater, first called on Professor Fansler?"

"Sure I remember; I told you about it. Get to the nub, man."

"Miss Fansler was stuck in the elevator that day, and kept you waiting."

"Not really. You seem to keep mentioning elevators. Have you noticed it? Look into it, man, that sort of thing can become serious."

Reed decided to ignore this disingenuous remark. "How many people knew you were going to talk to Professor Fansler, to ask for the first time to be officially admitted to a Graduate English class?"

"Everyone, man. We were like publicizing it. We'd had it with that boys' group always having us on the defensive —we told the world we were going to move, we announced our schedule of offensives. Your bird was the first."

"Professor Fansler," Reed said, frowning slightly, "was carefully picked for this offensive."

"Natch. We had to decide—old Vivian even consulted with some of us students before deciding which faculty member would be the best to begin on."

"Vivian?" Reed faintly said.

"Frogmore. We all came up with the name of your Professor Fansler, and we told the world. A compliment, really; don't get uptight about it."

"On the contrary," Reed said. "May I contribute," he asked, reaching into his pocket, "to the beer or cigarette supply?" In his day, Reed thought, such a request would have been considered insulting and patronizing; he would have been lucky to get away unassaulted. Because money was scarcer then? Or more sacred? Peabody's response was simple.

"That would be much appreciated," he said, "in these penniless parts." Reed handed over the money, and thought to himself as he walked back to the campus that money became desanctified only to those who had neither earned it nor done without it. The question was, was that a good or a bad thing?

So it *was* Cudlipp who had started the elevator business; madly to disrupt the University as the hated University College moved toward power? Only one more errand, Reed thought.

And he set his wandering feet on the path to the Dean's Office, now occupied, in the legal sense, by Robert O'Toole.

O'Toole was moving in and out of the Dean's Office like a reverse spectre—someone, that is, who haunts the place he is soon to inhabit. The Acting Dean was only too happy to vacate; indeed, his eagerness to depart the office bordered on the indecent. Kate was right: administrators were not going to be easily come by in the days that lay ahead.

Half expecting a snub, Reed was pleasantly surprised to find himself being ushered into O'Toole's office, offered a seat with a certain flourish, and encouraged to settle in for a cozy chat. Life was certainly very odd. But, as Kate had observed to Reed, the need to talk had markedly overcome many since the passage from the old life—and, to be sure, an unwillingness to chatter had never marked the academic profession.

"You have pleasant surroundings for your new and onerous tasks," Reed observed. The room was a lovely one, paneled, high-ceilinged, with the graciousness no new building, however elegant, could achieve.

"My main reaction to it," O'Toole said, "is a desire to run and not to stop till I hit some pleasant spot in the middle or far west."

"Surely there are no hiding places," Reed said.

"Obviously not. Have you noticed *The Times* is devoting a special section, complete with index, to the turmoil in the colleges? Perhaps we, like plague victims who have recovered, will be safest of all."

"I have often wondered if the carrying on with one's daily life is not the most difficult part: no excitement and glory, just plain hard work."

O'Toole nodded. "You want, I assume, to talk about Cudlipp's death."

"If you don't mind."

"I don't mind, but I can't help. The whole thing seemed so shocking, even in a place by now inured to shocks."

"You mean there is no inherent logic in the situation?"

"Yes," O'Toole said. "I guess that's what I mean."

Reed paused. "You are widely known as—I believe the word 'disciple' has actually been used—of Clemance. Is he as great a teacher as they say?"

"Absolutely great; almost *sui generis*, if you know what I mean, as though one had to judge him by special standards." O'Toole leaned back in his chair. "He taught us to think, those of us who came with the necessary equipment for thinking, which is rarer than you might suppose. We did not always draw the same conclusions he did, but he was a good enough teacher, even, to be pleased with that.

And then, so much of what he has himself produced is first-rate; some of it errs, but none of it is cheap. He has even written plays, which means he understands something of literary creation, but, most important, I am inclined to think, he is never esoteric, scholarly, or turgid. What he has to say is available to any cultured, intelligent man who will read with care. But I sound as though I were writing his obituary, which God forbid. When your teacher becomes your colleague, there is a tendency to think of him as two people: from then, and now."

"What of Cudlipp, whose obituary you could be writing?"

"Cudlipp was a more ordinary academic; an interesting scholar and a good teacher to those who could stand his rasping ways. Absolutely devoted to the College. I admire loyalty and devotion."

"What I've seen of your work seems very good to me," Reed said. "In the Clemance line: socially relevant discussions of literature with intimations of morality. Will you have time for work when you are dean?"

"I hope to have, but no doubt every new dean beguiles himself in that way. The secret, I suspect, is to be able to sleep only four hours a night."

"Let me ask you a pointed, not to say barbed, question, Mr. O'Toole. Do you intend to continue fighting, as Cudlipp did, the continued functioning of University College? I know you've told the Board of Governors and the administration that, as a new dean, you don't feel the Administrative Council should be allowed to so much as vote on expressing confidence in the University College until the mysteries surrounding Cudlipp's death are cleared up. But, should that . . ."

"As a matter of fact," O'Toole said, "I've changed my mind. To be frank, the pressure from the alumni of the College is enormous, but I'm inclined to think that we ought to let the vote go through; certainly we ought not to hold it up because of Cudlipp's death. There is really no question, is there? Cudlipp's death was an accident. It isn't as though he had been shot or anything. I admit that immediately after his death I was moved to follow a policy which he would have approved as a delaying tactic but— we are the living. The University must adopt the attitude that Cudlipp's death is a closed book; we must proceed to rebuild the University. I'm about to get in touch with Castleman and Klein and the Acting President and tell them."

Reed regarded O'Toole for a while. Kate's adjective for him had been arrogant, and Reed had learned to trust Kate's adjectives. But the man in front of him was not arrogant. "I think your change of mind is understand- able," Reed said, "and almost certainly best for the Uni- versity. Except, of course, that you have, by your previous attitude, stirred up a certain amount of investigation, and it is easier to begin these operations than to stop them."

"But surely there isn't anything to discover, is there?"

"There is the problem of the elevators."

"You mean, to the extent that the elevator stoppage was responsible for Cudlipp's death?"

"That stoppage, and others. Mr. O'Toole, I believe I know who was behind the interference with the elevators, but I would like confirmation; hunches have little legal standing. I'm looking for some College students, one, two, perhaps three. I wondered if you could help me to find them."

"I'm not even officially Dean yet."

"I know, and I apologize for importuning you so early, not to say prematurely, in your administrative career. I believe there are one or two young men who may, as a prank of course, perhaps rather radical youngsters . . ."

"Why do you think they're radical? Because only radi- cals do mischief?"

"No. Because they are students Hankster was particularly interested in. I may have drawn an incorrect conclusion. That, however, is not the point. All I want is a statement from those students of what they were doing, and assurances that it will stop. The whole matter need not go outside University disciplinary procedures, nor even that far if you do not choose."

"What makes you think I know who they are?"

"Perhaps, as the new dean, you can guess. Will you look into it and let me know? Is that a bargain?"

"You might call me in a day or two and see what I've decided," O'Toole said.

"All right, I will. Thank you for your help." Reed was amused and a little relieved to see the old arrogance returning. "I'll telephone tomorrow," he said. "And I do want to wish you all good fortune in your years as dean. You may be inaugurating an important new policy, where faculty members give a few years to administrative work out of devotion."

O'Toole stood up and, with great formality, bowed Reed from the room.

CHAPTER
ELEVEN

That fellow was back,
More bloody-minded than they remembered,
More godlike than they thought.

Kate and Reed met Clemance outside the auditorium. Clemance had succeeded in reserving three seats, and they were ushered, past glaring standees, to their places in the third row.

"I've had a word with Auden," Clemance said. "I suspect there's a good deal of kindness in his presence here; he knows a few of the students. He's going to read his poems and answer a few questions and then he's got to be off. So there's no chance of a party or anything for him afterward."

Here Auden was led onto the stage by the student head of the GSES. Kate could not think back to a day when so prominent a poet would not be introduced by someone at the University at least half as prominent in his own right. But achievement, these days, gave place to youth.

"We are honored and grateful," the student said, "to have Wystan Hugh Auden with us tonight to read his poems. He has said that after the reading he will answer a few questions if they are relevant." Auden's slight look of surprise at this suggested to Kate that this was a free translation of anything Auden might have said. But it received a grateful laugh soon followed, as the student sat down and Auden rose, by thunderous applause. "I mount the rostrum unafraid," he had written in a marvelously funny poem, "On the Circuit," which Kate found herself recalling with delight.

Auden read some recent poems, and some older poems, and a fairly recent poem to Miss Marianne Moore on her eightieth birthday: "It's much too muffled to say," he concluded, "how well and with what unfreckled integrity It has all been done."

"What a tribute to have earned," Clemance said to Kate, beneath the applause.

In the question-and-answer period which followed, Kate found herself remembering, not Auden's exact phrases, but their purport: no game can be played without rules. A secondary world must have its laws no less than a primary world. By "secondary world," Auden meant a work of art, but it occurred to Kate, thinking of the present university situation of turmoil, to wonder whether the secondary worlds the revolutionaries were trying to create were not, so far, dangerously lawless. Or did the young not realize the necessity of law? "Absolute freedom is meaningless," Auden said. One is free to decide what laws there shall be, but once imposed, they must be obeyed. A troubling thought applied to anything but art. And Kate remembered one other phrase of Auden's she had wanted repeatedly to quote to the young, though he had intended it only for poets: those who refuse all formal restrictions don't know what fun they're missing.

Auden concluded by saying that the life of a poet is a balancing act between frivolity and earnestness. Without the frivolity he is a bore, without the earnestness, an æsthete.

I must remember to tell that to Emilia Airhart, Kate thought; that, I shall say, is Auden's greatness; he is the best balancer of all.

"Will you come home for a drink?" Kate asked Clemance, when they again stood outside the auditorium. "I shall soon be leaving the apartment in which I have been very happy, and it seems to me that it would mark the formal closing of that happiness most fittingly if you would spend some time there."

"A most gracious invitation," Clemance said. "How fortunate you are to go from remembered happiness to anticipated happiness. Is it agreeable to you if I accept the invitation?" he asked Reed.

"Perfectly," Reed said. "Let's get a taxi."

Yet when they were all seated in Kate's living room, all supplied with spiritous liquors, Clemance seemed strangely silent. Kate spoke of Auden, of her thoughts during Auden's remarks on the need for law in secondary worlds.

"My mind was working much the same way," Clemance said. "I expect I was so drawn to literature from the beginning because it is the only way in which man can create worlds: his godlike faculty. The only mistake is not to understand the necessary distinction between the laws of the primary and secondary worlds—the primary world being, of course, the actual world we inhabit."

"Surely something of what we learn from literature can be used in life," Kate said. "Our greater awareness, if nothing else."

Another silence. Then Clemance said: "It begins to look as though your University College is to get a new lease on life. I have no doubt it will be given a vote of confidence by the Administrative Council, perhaps as its last act before the Faculty Senate takes over. A most significant act, I dare say. You must be feeling glad of that."

"I am, of course," Kate said. "But you do realize, don't you, that until the beginning of this term, I had never given the University College a single, wandering thought? I can't imagine how it became such a crusade with me, even if my help was sought out. I suspect I was outraged at those who didn't want their status symbols interfered with. I mean, it was so clear the fight wasn't over academic excellence, but over snobbery and a wicked kind of prejudice."

"I like the word 'wicked,'" Clemance said. "No doubt you realize, at least, and I'm certain as can be that Reed Amhearst realizes, that I've come tonight to talk about Cudlipp, the College, the whole mess. You *know*, don't you?" he said to Reed.

"Yes," Reed said. Kate stared at them.

"How did you guess?" Clemance asked. "Idle curiosity on my part, since I intended to tell you anyway. A process of elimination?"

"How could I have helped but guess?" Reed said. "Everything in your actions, afterward, made me certain. It was easy enough to guess you had done it, but how to know? Finally, it was a very slight thing that told me. That day we met you on the campus. I became so nervous when I knew I had the truth, I spoke to you idiotically about your daughter."

Clemance listened, with what those who do not understand like to call an academic interest.

"Everyone else," Reed went on, "in discussing the aspirin, spoke of them as being somehow put into the tube in which Cudlipp carried his British pills. Everyone assumed the substitution had been made in his supply. But you, in speaking to Kate and me, referred to the person who had 'handed' Cudlipp the aspirin. I knew, of course, that they had to have been handed to him; no other method would have worked. And you handed them to him, right in front of Kate's eyes. I don't think, even at the end, that Cudlipp suspected you. He, too, I'm certain, thought it was an accident; something that had gone wrong at the source."

"I never meant to kill him. Need I say that?"

"I never for a moment thought you did," Reed said.

"We cannot guess the outcome of our actions—how often I have said that in discussions with students. Which is why our actions must always be acceptable in themselves, and not as strategies. Kant put it differently and better."

"It is most unusual for aspirin to kill that way. And then there was the complication of the elevator."

"Neither did I think," Clemance went on, as though he had not heard, "that the crime would be laid at the feet, so to speak, of the University College. It's strange, really, how that seemed so germane to it all, and yet had nothing to do with it."

"Not in your mind. But Cudlipp's actions against the University College must have gone some way toward making you realize the strangeness of Cudlipp's behavior. He was mad, wasn't he, or near so?"

"Oh yes," Clemance said. "At the end I think he was probably certifiably mad. But who was to certify him, or even, if it came to that, to notice, till the damage was done? A number of faculty actually cracked, you know, under the strain of last spring's events; it took different people different ways. One extremely prominent member of the faculty, whom Kate probably heard, ranted on to his colleagues one night in a completely vile and incoherent way. It was assumed by most people that he was drunk. But he wasn't drunk. He suffered, not from alcohol, but from fatigue and psychic strain."

Kate rose to fetch them all fresh drinks.

"Cudlipp, alas," Clemance went on, "had cracked up. This anti-University College mania—he actually organized some students to stop elevators—was only a minor symptom, really. He was becoming paranoiac and utterly power-mad. He persuaded Robert O'Toole to become Dean of the College. Oh, I know what you must think—that I was jealous that Robert transferred his devotion from me to Cudlipp—but if I was jealous, that was only a small part of it. Cudlipp was corrupting O'Toole, as he was corrupting others. Not that it will matter if O'Toole is Dean for a while now. I imagine he may even do some good.

"What you must try to realize is the great affection I had for Cudlipp—years of affection and admiration before he went to pieces. It took me a good while to face up to the truth about him. And then I had to decide what to do. Some action was clearly necessary. He couldn't be allowed to go on. He wouldn't take a leave, take any time off. But I hoped, if he were ill and forced to take a leave of absence, he might reconsider, recover, return to his former self, or some new-found self. His marriage was wrecked, you know, along with everything else. I tried to talk to his wife, but she assured me that he was sick and past being reached by any means she knew of.

"I had known for years about the aspirin. It was never suggested, by Cudlipp or anyone else, that aspirin could be fatal. Such a possibility never occurred to me. But we are not gods, and the laws of our primary world inevitably operate. I hoped Cudlipp would be immobilized for a time, given time to think, made ill, perhaps frightened into reconsidering. I don't want to suggest I wasn't aware of the seriousness of what I was doing, but I had to act. I waited until a day when he had a new supply of pills, so that there could be no question of suspecting anyone; so my essentially non-criminal mind worked. Funny, isn't it?"

"Do you mean," Kate said, "that I watched you hand Cudlipp those aspirin?"

"Yes, you did. Your party, as it turned out, provided the perfect chance which I had not found earlier that day. I am so terribly sorry that I did not properly think how I might affect . . ."

"Don't worry about that," Kate said. "As you realized, that party was none of Reed's or my doing, but rather an aboriginal celebration of a marriage rite. But I keep trying to think back to the moment when you brought the soda water . . ."

"Yes. I had a bottle of soda water in one hand and a glass in the other. Cudlipp was holding his pills in one hand and the University College catalogue in the other. I put down the bottle of soda water and took the pills from him, handing him the glass instead. Then I filled the glass with soda water, and handed him back the pills as he put down the catalogue. It sounds complicated and intricate, like a ballet or conjuring trick, but it was ridiculously easy. Had it turned out not to be, I should simply not have gone ahead with the substitution. As it was, the pills I handed him were two ordinary aspirin. I knew they were dangerous for him; I never thought they could be lethal."

"Buffered aspirin, as it turned out," Reed said. "So that he did not immediately taste the aspirin and spit them out."

"My God," Clemance said. "I never thought of that. It does sound a diabolic scheme. They were simply the kind of aspirin I use. No doubt," he added, "a good prosecuting lawyer could make much of that."

They were all silent for a moment.

"I cannot see," Reed said, "that there need be a prosecuting lawyer, or a trial. Had I thought the possibility of such a trial existed, I should not have allowed this conversation to take place. Perhaps," Reed added, "this is the nearest I shall ever come to creating a secondary world."

"No doubt it will sound unbearably pompous and unsuitable coming from me, but I cannot add to murder the sin of allowing you to be party to a crime."

"What better way to celebrate my marriage to Nancy Drew and my probable departure from the D.A.'s Office?" Reed smiled. "No," he said, "I would do neither of us any favor to cover any of this up. But we need not publicize it.

I shall introduce into the file an account of how you must have given Cudlipp the aspirin; an accident will be assumed, and indeed, his death was an accident if I know the definition of the word.

"You have nothing to fear from anyone but yourself. If I might presume to persuade you of anything, it is to try to find the courage to continue in your work. You are essential to your university, and your instincts about Cudlipp were all correct. I do admit, however, that I have used a certain amount of blackmail to establish the truth of Cudlipp's tricks with the elevators, and to save students from such further nonsense."

"With O'Toole, I suppose?"

"Yes. He will produce the students. And in his work as Dean, he will need your support and help."

"Did he guess?"

"Yes. No doubt of it. I was certain as soon as I heard of his intention to call off his demands for forestalling the University College. He still admires you, you know, and I think, was not a little concerned about Cudlipp himself."

"If you want," Kate said, "in the old moral way, to pay a price, remember that the University College is now almost certainly assured of continued existence and development. Perhaps that is not something you would have wished for."

"You wished for it," Clemance said. "It will be my wedding present. I hope I find the courage to continue my work. As to the price I pay, you need never concern yourselves about the appropriate enormity of that."

CHAPTER TWELVE

Clio,
Muse of Time, but for whose merciful silence
Only the first step would count and that
Would always be murder, whose kindness never
Is taken in, forgive our noises
And teach us our recollections.

By the middle of November, the evenings were drawing in. The campus was almost dark by the time the offices closed and the secretaries went home. Kate, walking in the dusk toward the subway, was again visited by this sense of—what did one call it, affection, love, devotion?—and again wondered: toward what do I feel this sense of loyalty, a quite out-of-date emotion? Kate, in a way, sympathized with the younger generation who considered loyalty a typical demand of the establishment. Loyalty, after all, like patriotism, is the last refuge of scoundrels. Yet how explain this love? Suffice it perhaps to say that here was an institution for which she would willingly work; the University was not, for her, simply a place wherein to pursue a career. I recognize the claim, she thought, even if I cannot recognize what it is that makes the claim.

The University College had been affirmed in its existence. It had won the credit to be a full-fledged undergraduate college in a first-rate university, though certainly it had achieved this status by a strange route. "Dare sound authority confess," Auden's poem asked, "that one can err his way to riches, win glory by mistake?" Well, Clio had known.

Meanwhile, academia ground on its way.

Professor Peter Packer Pollinger, to the amazement and delight of everyone, brought out a book on Fiona Macleod with such insight into the odd dual nature of William Sharp that Professor Pollinger's colleagues looked at him with new attention. But he continued to puff through his mustache and grew, if anything, more vague and petulant. He delighted Kate by informing her one day that he had been reading the poetry of Sara Teasdale and that it was perfectly obvious no such person had ever existed. She was the alter ego of Vachel Lindsay. He had made a profound study of their imagery and was prepared to defend his thesis.

"I don't suppose," he said, puffing, "that you know *her* poem about the daisies and the asters."

"As a matter of fact," Kate smilingly said, "I do."

"Well, you see," Professor Pollinger went on," the secret's there. Daisies and asters are both carduaceous plants, having, that is, discordant and radiate heads. But one appears to supply simple answers and the other shares its name with a biological phenomenon of achromatic substance found in cells which divide themselves by mitosis."

"They do?" Kate said. "I mean, it does?"

"Naturally. The aster originated in China, that is to say the Orient, never hot for certitude but full of the rhythm of life. The daisy originated in Europe, with its chief religions of simple answers and the simplistic beauty of its natural world. Both sides of the same person."

"But," Kate began, "there is a great deal of clear evidence that . . ."

"Have you had your wedding yet?"

"No," Kate said. "Not yet."

. . .

Kate met Polly Spence for lunch at the Cosmo Club. "Buffet now, dear," Polly had said, "so get there early or all those vigorous ladies will have grabbed the tables."

Kate entered the Club like a revenant returning to an earlier life. When she had been a girl and it had not occurred to her or any member of her generation to refuse to go to all the benefit dances arranged for boys and girls from the proper schools, she had come to the Cosmopolitan Club where, somehow, they were always held. She remembered the steps down, after one had entered, to the ladies' room on the left where she and a couple of girls from Chapin and Sacred Heart had hidden out during almost all of one dance; she remembered the balconies, and the library where no one ever went.

"The library's changed, of course," Polly Spence said, when Kate had mentioned this, "all the latest books circulating like mad. They put me on the library committee and I said, 'Let's keep it old and stuffy and the way it always has been, where superannuated students like me can come and have a peaceful hour,' but activity is the order of the day, even here. Busy, busy. And what is your news, dear? When is the wedding to be? Why not have it here? Perfect."

"It's to be on Thanksgiving, with no one but two witnesses and a judge friend of Reed's."

Polly Spence sighed. "I remember your brothers' weddings," she said. "St. Thomas's and everything just so."

"That was never my style, you know, even in those days."

"I dare say. But you have done well, I think. You must bring your Reed to dinner and he and Winthrop can talk about all those dreary things lawyers always do talk about, and I can tell you about my wonderful new job."

"Tell me now."

"I don't dare, because it hasn't *absolutely* come through yet. But I'm so pleased. Imagine starting to teach linguis-

tics at my advanced age—I'm really considered a coming
scholar, even if I'll be gone before I've finally come. And
I'm so excited about University College. We're actually
beginning to get tenure for people. Do you suppose this
spring we'll be at the barricades again, filthy language,
long nights, and all the *desperate* excitement of revolution?"

"My opinion, for what it's worth, is that we won't.
Some other places may be, though. You know, the only
thing I really remember about the Cosmopolitan Club,
apart from the dances for the benefit of blue babies or
whatever it was, are the macaroons. Do they still have
those fantastically good macaroons?"

"Certainly they do, my dear, though now, of course,
one serves oneself. Winthrop says pretty soon they'll be
selling a mix for them, and they will begin to taste like
the glue on postage stamps, but I tell him not to be such
a confirmed pessimist. I really do think life is just too
wonderfully exciting, especially now that I don't have to
look after grandchildren anymore. My children point out
that *I* was able to hire governesses, and I point out that *I*
never contradicted my mother, but after all, *autre temps,
autre moeurs, n'est-ce-pas?*"

"And what do they say to that?" Kate asked, munching
macaroons.

"They don't say much, dear, but they glare, and I know
what they're thinking: four-letter-word-sex you, meaning
me, of course. *Tant pis.*"

For Clemance, Kate felt an aching need to offer comfort
and knew no comfort existed on earth.

"There is," he told her, "a terrible need to demand
punishment—to punish oneself. Resign, retire, go quietly
and miserably mad in a richly deserved and dreary solitude. We never know, these psychological days, when we
are fooling ourselves, but it seems to me that since I

destroyed Cudlipp for the sake of the young men in the College, I ought to stay to serve those same young men—those, at least, who care for what I say. Yet, you know, it seems to me there is never a half hour together when I do not re-live that moment of handing him the aspirin."

"And how," Professor Castleman said as he and Kate waited for the elevator in Lowell Hall, "is the proclaimer?"

"The who?" Kate asked.

"Clio, your muse of history. Kleio in Greek is the Proclaimer."

"You don't say. I never thought of her as proclaiming, I suppose because Auden never mentioned it."

The elevator, going down, passed them without stopping.

"If your Clio is going to proclaim any change," Castleman said as they started down the stairs, "I wish she would begin. The elevators do not stop, and the room I'm in now, while larger, is still not large enough."

"Standing-room-only is a compliment," Kate said.

"Which reminds me. We went to the theater again. Dionysian rites, as I live and breathe. Nude young women pretending to tear nude young men to pieces. Oceans of blood."

"Did they try to persuade you to take part?"

"Alas, no. Not, that is, that I actually want to tear anyone apart—not even my students, bless them, who refuse to believe one can learn from history. Do you suppose," he went on, "if we were all to enter the classroom nude—and Lord knows, it's overheated enough for that—the younger generation might be willing to pay their tribute to Clio?"

Kate met Emilia Airhart in the ladies' room, where she was regarding herself miserably in the mirror.

"My plan," she said, "was always to avoid mirrors, the sight was so demoralizing. Do you know, I had actually learned to put on lipstick and comb my hair without looking at myself? But I will escape no longer. I am going to look and look and perhaps the continual shock will actually force me to diet. I will never be willowy, but at least I can be slightly angular."

Kate smiled. "You are probably no one's idea of either Aphrodite or Artemis, but you are wonderfully you and I doubt, really, that you ought to consider changing. The trouble with Queen Victoria was not her figure but her opinions. Are you writing a new play?"

"I am, actually. It's a comedy with supernatural bits. A community of middle-aged parents and teen-aged children, and they change places—keeping, of course, their original ideas. The result is that the colleges and prep schools become frightfully proper and *comme-il-faut*, but the banks and brokerage houses keep having disruptions, and the different partners keep occupying their Wall Street law firms. Meanwhile, on the floor of the exchange, the radical brokers take over the ticker tape and demand open admission for all seats on the exchange. Of course, the college students insist that any broker who interferes with the workings of the market will lose his right to a capital gains . . ."

Cartier would not stop long enough to talk. "Have you heard," Kate asked him, "that they have found the students who caused the elevator trouble?"

"I did hear something," Cartier said, fairly dancing to be gone. "Sorry, but I must prepare a class." He rushed off and then, to Kate's astonishment, allowed the strings of restlessness to twitch him back.

"Hope you will sit on my lap one day," he said, and then was gone.

EPILOGUE

Our bodies cannot love:
But, without one,
What works of Love could we do?

Kate and Reed were married on Thanksgiving and, since she had only four days, and a class to teach on Monday, they spent their honeymoon in Reed's apartment cooking all their meals in the electric frying pan, which required very little attention.

More Deadly, Delectable Detection from Virago

THE WHITE HAND
Jean Warmbold

A gripping political thriller of double-dealings, death squads and international intrigue

On Christmas morning a brutal murder takes place. The victim: a young woman cold-bloodedly shot down by two professional hit men. The accomplices: two local cops. The witness: Sarah Calloway, investigative reporter. This gruesome encounter plunges Sarah headlong into a perilous maze of double-dealings and international intrigue. Is she dealing with paramilitary drug smugglers? Nicaraguan Contras? Central American death squads? Or are there elements more insidious and closer to home? The truth which eventually surfaces is far more chilling than Sarah could ever have imagined: the terrifying reality of *Mano Blanca*, The White Hand.

CHILDREN'S GAMES
Janet LaPierre

Romance, blackmail and murder on the Californian coast

In Janet LaPierre's supremely atmospheric mystery, schoolteacher Meg Halloran and her young daughter Katy move to a small town to start a new life. Soon Meg receives anonymous letters and suspects they originate from her former student, religious fanatic Dave Tucker. Dave accuses Meg of making sexual advances, and when he's found murdered, his father, a prominent banker, and many of the townspeople are convinced Meg is responsible. Her reputation and livelihood at stake, Meg, with the sympathetic support of Police Chief Gutierrez, strives to clear her name. Her enquiries uncover shocking and unsavoury secrets. But for Katy's survival and her own, she persists in finding the killer.

Also by Janet LaPierre

THE CRUEL MOTHER

A tense psychological thriller where people and their plans collide in terrifying ways . . .

A dying sixties radical yearns for a last glimpse of his daughter. A wild fifteen-year-old plots to run away with her rich-kid boyfriend. What Meg Halloran and policeman Vince Gutierrez desire is a peaceful vacation together where Gutierrez can complete his recovery from a bullet wound. But on a highway in northern Idaho, people and their plans collide, rebound and regroup in terrifying ways. With no warning, Meg finds herself fighting for her own survival and that of a sullen teenage girl she doesn't like and cannot trust, while a battered Vince searches frantically for both of them.

THE DOG COLLAR MURDERS
Barbara Wilson

'Someone screamed, very loudly, "You've *all* killed her!"'

Loie Marsh, prominent anti-pornography activist, is found strangled by a dog collar at a Seattle conference on sexuality. The clues point to any number of suspects and it's up to Pam Nilsen, the printer-sleuth of Barbara Wilson's earlier mysteries, *Murder in the Collective* and *Sisters of the Road*, to find the killer. Was it someone who wanted to prevent Loie from speaking on her panel? The local lesbian sadomasochists? Feminist activists opposed to censorship, or Loie's ex-lover and former research collaborator? Or someone from Loie's distant past? In investigating Loie's death, Pam begins to come to terms with some of her own fears and desires. Meanwhile the murderer is still at large and strikes again . . .

MURDER BEHIND LOCKED DOORS
Ellen Godfrey

A gripping murder mystery in the cutthroat world of computers, technology and takeovers

Jane Tregar works at a large headhunting firm, finding top executives to fill high-powered jobs. Competent and successful, she nonetheless finds working in this overridingly male world as taxing as the 'constant speaking of a foreign language'. When the vice-president of a large software company is found dead in a locked computer room, Jane is asked to find a replacement. But suspicion surrounds his death and, worse still, the only suspects are the other five on the management team. When Jane's own life is threatened as she unravels the mystery, she is forced to recognise that values like loyalty have little currency where corporate manipulation and personal ambition are involved.

BEYOND HOPE
Eve Zaremba

'A fast-paced thriller . . . the one-liners alone are worth the trip'
– Margaret Atwood

A sixties revolutionary, Sara Ann Raymond, the daughter of a right-wing US presidential candidate, has been missing for ten years. She has recently been spotted working on a road-gang in the interior of British Columbia. What seems at first like a simple chore in vacation-land for Helen Keremos, lesbian detective, turns out to be her most complicated and terrifying case. Tracking down Sara Ann through the beautiful and remote mountains and valleys, Helen encounters an unlikely crew of people: an ex-draft resister, radical feminists, Doukhobor farmers and construction workers, a lumberjack . . . plus assorted agents, spies, arms smugglers, mobsters, cops . . . not to mention a dog. All are involved one way or another in a deadly game of multinational terrorism, murder and intrigue just forty miles from the Canadian-US border.

Also by Eve Zaremba

WORK FOR A MILLION

'Six minutes is not long . . . but it's plenty long enough to kill'

Soni Deerfield is a talented performer just hitting it big in the music biz, a recent million dollar lottery winner and a beautiful woman. Lucky Sonia. Or is she? For someone among her nearest and dearest is out to get her. Someone is conducting a harassment campaign of threatening phone calls, vandalism, minor accidents . . . Helen Keremos, susceptible as ever, falls under the spell of the red-haired millionaire, and is persuaded to take on the case. Within days simple harassment explodes into murder. And Helen needs all her street sus to untangle the chains of intrigue which are binding Sonia.